The
Druid Stone

"I will say my goodbye here then," he said, "since you have been so gracious as to come to me."

He took her by the shoulders and kissed her on the cheek. I saw her cling to him momentarily longer than he held her and then she said unsteadily, "And how many of those will you bestow on the girls of Morach before you go, Roddie?"

He laughed down at her. "I bestow them only where they give pleasure," he said.

"And they give pleasure to Kirsty?" she said.

Roddie smiled. "I should hope so," he said. "Kirsty and I are old friends."

"Indeed?" said Charlotte. "Only that?"

I saw a spark fly between them before she laughed and turned to lead the way back to the churchyard. I was about to speak, to ask Roddie why he had denied our love, but he put a finger gently on my lips and said softly, "Only trust me, Kirsty, and take care while I am away," and his lips brushed mine, feather-light, before he led me after Charlotte.

The
Druid Stone

Helen Magee

PIP
POLLINGER IN PRINT

Pollinger Limited
9 Staple Inn
Holborn
LONDON
WC1V 7QH

www.pollingerltd.com

First published by Scholastic 1998
This large print edition published by Pollinger in
Print 2007

A CIP catalogue record is available from the
British Library

ISBN 978-1-905665-63-1

Chapter 1

All my life I had been fascinated by the Druid A Stone. It stood on a small island in the middle of the loch, just visible amid a ring of oaks. Legend had it that those oaks were magical and descended from the sacred oaks of the Druidic religion which had once flourished in this part of Scotland. My mother, a practical woman, scoffed at such stories. But I was not so sure, for that was the only place where oak trees grew in our wind-blasted glen.

My mother was a lowlander and I had always been puzzled by the marriage between herself and my father. He had been a big, gentle man with the lilt of the Highlands in his voice. It was two years to the day since he had died and I had come to the churchyard with an offering of wild flowers for his grave.

Father had been ghillie to the Big House, or, to give it its proper title, Blair Morach, ancestral seat of the Munros of Morach and the Loch, a wild country of peatbog and moor. I had never set foot in the place though I had heard tales enough of the splendour of the balls and shooting parties that had once taken place there. That was when the Family had still lived there, before I was born.

It still hurt to think of my father, of the way he would say on a fine morning: "Well, lass, get your boots and it's out on the moor you'll go with me today." And I would pull on heavy boots and Mother would make up thick slices of bread and crowdie cheese and we'd be off the whole day with the sun on our backs and the springy turf beneath our feet. I knew it was not always like that for him, for there were days when the rain lashed the hills and the peat fires burned bright in the crofts and he would say: "No moor for you today, Kirsty. You stay and help your mother with the baking."

It was on such a day that he came home coughing, with a pain in his chest. Pneumonia, the doctor said, and, with incredible swiftness, he was gone. Too many years on the moor in all weathers.

My mother began to grow a little greyer and more careful of the pennies. She had always been a practical woman and she put her talents as a seamstress to good use, but making ends meet was not easy and we missed the presence of my father. There had not been much laughter in the house since he had died.

At first the neighbours were kindness itself and I would be called in to a croft and given a newly baked scone and a glass of milk or slipped a penny "for yourself, lass". But I soon learned to refuse such offers after Mother found out.

"You are not a beggar," she said, her face white with anger.

"But it's not like that, Mother," I protested. "They're sorry for us. They just want to be kind."

"I don't want their pity," she said. "Nor their charity, Kirsty."

"But Roddie MacLelland is in and out of houses getting scones and milk all the time. He even boasts about it," I said.

She drew herself up and I was afraid of what I had said.

"And are you comparing yourself with Roddie MacLelland now? A boy who hasn't boots to his name that aren't two sizes too big for him, or a shirt on his back that hasn't been on someone else's?"

"He can't help being poor, Mother," I said. "He only has his grandmother and she's quite old. There's no man in the house."

"Nor ever has been," she snapped.

"His parents are dead," I said.

"His mother is dead," she replied. "As for his father – who's to know?"

"What do you mean?" I said, puzzled.

She put her hand to her mouth. "Nothing, child, nothing," she said. "But you must have

3

nothing to do with Roddie MacLelland. You are different. You're too young to understand. Just promise me you will stay away from him."

"But Father used to take him out on the moor sometimes – and on the loch where he never took me," I cried.

She looked suddenly tired and bent towards me, putting her arms round me in an unaccustomed gesture.

"Kirsty," she said quietly, "your father was a good man with a kind heart, sometimes too kind a heart. This was his home. He had known the MacLellands all his life. It's different for us now. Don't try to understand. Just do as I ask."

I opened my mouth to protest but closed it again as I saw the weariness in her face, and instead I gave her a kiss.

"All right, Mother. I'll do as you ask," I said. But my heart sank at the word – the words that seemed to follow me now: we were different.

It wasn't easy avoiding Roddie. It wasn't easy avoiding anybody in Morach but I tried, though my heart wasn't in it. I liked Roddie despite his threadbare shirts and his big Boots. He was kind and he had loved my father I think almost as much as I had – though, of course, he would never have admitted to that. The most he said when Father died was: "I'll miss him too, Kirsty. And if there's peats needing dug or heavy work to be done, I'll be there."

I had looked at him, tall already for his fourteen years and broad in the shoulder, but thin despite the scones he seemed to consume in such quantities.

"Thanks, Roddie," I said. "I'll remember."

But of course I never did ask him for help, not after what Mother had said.

He caught up with me one day as we were coming home from school.

"Kirsty," he said, "you'll come up the hill tomorrow, will you not? I've something to show you."

His eyes were alight with excitement and I found myself on the brink of saying yes before I remembered my mother. I couldn't meet his eyes.

"I can't," I said. "I have to help my mother with the baking."

"Well, when you've done," he said easily. "It'll not take all day to do a bit of baking. I've found a plover's nest. I want you to see the eggs."

I looked at my toes. "I can't," I said again. Then I couldn't help but look at him. His hair was very dark against the whiteness of his face and his eyes very blue, with none of their characteristic light left in them.

"Then I was right," he said. "You *have* been avoiding me."

I couldn't answer.

"Why, Kirsty?" he said, a bit more softly now. "Why?"

I couldn't speak except to say, "My mother. . ." Then I couldn't go on.

His eyes grew hard again. "Aye," he said. "I've heard you want help from no one. But I didn't realize that meant you didn't want friendship either."

"It's not that," I said. "It's just that. . ."

"Just that what?" he said.

"It's . . . she. . ." I stammered.

I saw understanding dawn in his eyes and his mouth twisted in a bitter smile as he said, "Your father thought I was good enough for you, Kirsty. And there was no finer man in Morach. I'll say goodbye, Miss Strachan." And he turned on his heel and strode away.

I stood there in misery for a moment before turning homeward. I knew now what Mother had against him. It hadn't been hard to find out. It was common knowledge, and the wonder of it was that I hadn't known before. He was illegitimate, though some called it by another name. His mother had died when he was an infant. People hinted that his father had been a local man who had left the village years ago. But I couldn't see that it mattered very much who Roddie's father was or why it should stop me being friends with him. I wished with all my heart that my father was still alive to explain it to me.

That was the first time I turned my steps towards the churchyard and sat looking out to the Druid Island, missing my father's wisdom and kindness.

The first time but not the last time. Now here I was again, on the anniversary of his death, and the pain was no more bearable. I thought I would not be disturbed for it was a great day in Morach. The Laird had returned after an absence of many years and most of the villagers were up at the castle waiting to welcome him. But I *was* disturbed.

I was so engrossed in my thoughts that I barely heard the footsteps. I turned and looked up into Roddie's face.

"Did you know that you're crying?" he said gently.

I wiped the tears away hastily. "No," I said. "I didn't."

"I saw the flowers," he said.

"You remembered?"

"Why wouldn't I? He was good to me," Roddie said simply as he sat down beside me. "He would have liked us to be friends, Kirsty."

"I know," I said. "But Mother. . ."

"Aye, well," he said with a smile. "We needn't flaunt it. Just so you and I know there's friendship between us".

I felt as if a great weight had been lifted from me.

"I'd like that, Roddie," I said and it was settled. Not a secret friendship but not a blatant one either.

"You were looking at the Druid Island," he said.

I looked out towards it once more. "I've always wanted to see the Druid Stone," I said, "and stand under those oak trees. I've always thought there was a mystery about them."

"The Druids were here long before Christianity came," he said. "And they had some strange customs. Sacrifices, they say, were made on the Druid Stone." His eyes darkened. "There are still some strange customs associated with the island."

"What customs? You make it sound frightening," I said.

"Just silly nonsense," he said. "Somebody came to the village years ago and wrote a book about them." His mouth tightened. "Made half of them up, I dare say. But the Druids were different. I suppose it is frightening in a way to think of something so strong dying so completely."

"Everything dies," I said.

He looked at me quickly. "Sorry, Kirsty," he said. "That was a stupid thing to say." He ran a hand through his hair. "First I frighten you, then I upset you," he said.

I smiled at his forlorn look. "It's all right," I said. I hesitated. "You don't like the Druid Island, do you?" I asked.

Roddie turned away. "No," he said. "But I'll take you out to it and you can touch the oaks and see they're just trees like any others and there's nothing to be frightened of."

I leapt up, then stopped. "But what would my mother say?"

His eyes shone with devilment. "She'll be up at the House."

I laughed. "How do you know?"

"Half the village is up at the House getting work of some kind now that the Laird is back," he replied.

"And why not you?" I asked.

He looked at me levelly. "I have other plans," he said. "The Dominie says I've tae stick tae ma books and I'll mebbe get a scholarship tae the University." His voice had dropped in a perfect imitation of the schoolmaster's and I laughed.

"And what will you do at the University?" I said, thinking it a great joke.

His face was turned away from me, looking at the island. "I'm going to be a lawyer," he said.

I felt my jaw drop in amazement. He was perfectly serious.

"But that'll take years!" I said. "Your grandmother. . ."

He turned back to me and I caught a glimpse of the man this boy, in his patched shirt and worn boots, would become.

"I'm not forgetting her," he said.

I looked at him. "I'm sorry I didn't take you seriously," I said.

He smiled. "You're not the only one that won't take me seriously," he replied. "But I'll not let that bother me. Now, pick up your skirts and I'll show you my boat."

He turned away and I was left to follow. It hadn't even occurred to me to wonder how we would get to the island. Whether it was the Druid Stone or the University, if Roddie MacLelland decided to go, then go he would. But my confidence faltered a little when I saw the boat.

"It's got more patches than my boots," I said.

"And do your boots let in the water?" he asked as he heaved it over and began to drag it across the shingle towards the water.

"No," I said.

"And neither does this boat," he said. "In you get."

I did. There really was nothing else to do.

"Where did you get it?" I asked as he pushed off and jumped in beside me.

"From your father," he said. "It was in need of mending and just lying around useless. I put a whole winter's work into this." He drew on the oars and smiled at me. "I'd call it *The Kirsty* but that would draw attention, so I'll call it *The Friendship*."

"I thought we were going to the island," I said. "You're heading away from it."

He cast a glance over his shoulder. "You can't make straight for it," he said. "A current from the river runs into the loch and if you got caught in that you'd be in trouble. It's an undertow, you see, and not visible on the surface, so you can only get to the island if you approach it in a wide sweep from the other side. That's how the legend started about the island repelling strangers."

"You know a lot about this island," I said.

"I've talked to the Dominie about it," Roddie said. "He has a great interest in history."

"And you're his best scholar," I said. "You always have been."

He cocked his head on one side. "Ach, I'm no sae bad," he said – again in perfect imitation of the Dominie.

"Don't you let him hear you do that," I said, "or he'll be after you with the tawse for all you're bigger than he is now."

He laughed. "Well, it wouldn't be the first time he's belted me," he said.

"For fighting mostly," I replied.

"I'm done with fighting now," he said. "Or at least fighting with the fists. There's other kinds of fighting to be done now."

"To get to the University?" I said.

He looked at me and his face was quite serious for a moment.

"That as well," he said. Then, before I could ask him what he meant, "Did you see them arriving?"

I didn't have to ask what he meant by that. The glen had been buzzing with the news for weeks.

"I did that," I said. "I was up the glen when the carriages arrived at the House. I've never seen anything like it. They fairly put Hamish MacCrimmon's pony and trap to shame."

We both laughed. Hamish owned the only shop in the village and the only pony and trap for that matter and he was very proud of it. It was a great occasion when Hamish went into Fort William to get provisions for his shop and take in anyone who wanted to get something special from the big shops.

"Four horses to a carriage," I said. "And a coat of arms on the side. And did you see the people? A man – that'll be the Laird, I suppose – and a boy and girl who can't be much older than us. And did you see the hat she was wearing? Feathers on it and a bird I've never seen the like of. Oh, it was wonderful!"

"And what would your mother say if she caught you gawping at the gentry?" said Roddie, laughing at me.

"She gawped herself," I said, "when she went up to get her place. Mrs Robertson – you know, the housekeeper that's been up there all these years with Effie and Ewan all on their own – she's opened up the whole house now. The things Mother saw – chandeliers and pictures and – oh, it's just wonderful!"

"Your mother's got her place in the house now?" said Roddie.

"Och, there was no trouble about that," I said. "Didn't Father work for the estate all his life and his father before him? And besides, she's a very good seamstress."

"And you, Kirsty," Roddie said. "Will you be going for a place?"

We were almost at the island now. I looked towards it, afraid I might laugh. "No," I said. "Mother says I've to stay at the school and maybe become a schoolteacher myself one day."

His laughter rocked the boat as it grated on the sandy shore of the island.

"Oh Kirsty," he said, handing me out. "And isn't it ambitious that we are?"

I laughed back at him. "We might have ambitions," I said, "but we still have patches on our boots."

He dragged the boat up on the shore and we turned towards the middle of the island. It wasn't large but it sloped quite steeply down to the water.

"Did you hear why they came back?" I said. "There are all sorts of stories going round."

"They say the Laird's wife died," said Roddie. "She was English and never wanted to live here, or so the story goes."

"How long is it since the Laird lived here?" I said.

I was almost at the top of the slope and Roddie stood for a moment above me, outlined against the light.

"Many a long year, Kirsty," he said. "Since before we were born, anyway. He was a young man when he left Morach, then he married an English wife and never came back." His eyes were dark with an expression I could not read. Then he shook his head. "But that is all past history," he said. "He's back now and Morach has a laird again. Now, let's look at this island of yours."

Chapter 2

I moved to stand beside Roddie on the rise that formed a rim around the middle of the island. The grass below us was short and springy, like moss, but it was the oaks that tugged at my imagination. They stood in a perfect circle, like sentinels guarding a holy place, and in the centre was the Druid Stone. The stone was not large, nor was it carved or dressed in any way, but it looked so completely right, so fitting in that place that it made me shiver slightly. I had the feeling that to break the circle of the trees and walk on that ring of grass would be intrusive somehow, and would bring bad luck.

My hand went out to steady myself and I felt the warm roughness of bark beneath it and it seemed to me that a kind of peace flowed through me from the oak tree. I looked up through its fresh green leaves towards the sky and thought – but of course! These trees have not always been here. They are descendants of more ancient oaks. It's the stone that has always been here. My eyes were drawn once again to the centre of the circle. Then Roddie held out his hand to me and drew me through the trees and, as we stepped on the grass, a rabbit scuttled across our path.

"That explains why the grass is so short," I said, and the spell was broken.

We advanced towards the stone. It was oddly regular in shape for a stone that was so obviously natural and uncut, and the top was flat, broad and smooth to the touch.

"Do you know any more of the legends?" I asked.

"Apart from the usual stories that grow up about a place like this?" he said. "Well, there's the one I told you about – the legend that the island won't let strangers land on it. But that has a perfecdy natural explanation. It's the current in the loch, not the island. Then there are always stories of human sacrifices—"

I gasped and he smiled.

"But I wouldn't put too much faith in those," he said. He drew his hand across the stone. "Some say in the past it was a healing stone."

"You mean sick people were brought here and made well?"

"You musn't believe all the stories, Kirsty," he said. "This was a hundred, maybe two hundred years ago when there was no road into the glen and no doctor either."

I sighed. I would have quite liked to have thought of the place as good rather than sinister as I had felt when I stood beyond the circle of trees.

"What else?" I said.

"Years ago, when there was no minister in the glen, they say the young people would come to the island and walk round the Druid Stone together before spending a night on the island," he said. "Then they were considered married."

"You sound as if you don't approve of the idea," I said. He didn't answer and I went on. "Was that in the book you were talking about – the book about Morach?"

"It was," he said. "But it was my grandmother that first told me about the custom. It doesn't happen any longer."

"It must be a long time since it's been done," I said.

"Within living memory," he said. Then, "My mother and father did it."

"Your father?" I blurted out, turning to him. "Then they *were* married!"

He flushed. "After a fashion," he said.

His mouth set in a firm line and I knew the subject was closed. I gazed at him, standing there, his eyes bright with anger. Then he turned quickly.

"Do you hear something?" he said.

I listened. Faintly, from beyond the trees on the landward side of the island, I heard voices upraised.

"Let's see who it is," I said, starting towards the sound.

Roddie was before me as we scrambled up the farther rim and I heard him curse softly.

"The fools!" he said. "They'll kill themselves."

I struggled up beside him. "What is it?" I said as I looked across the water. Then I saw what he was looking at. Two people, a boy and a girl by the looks of it, had just launched themselves in a little boat on to the loch and were making straight for the island. The girl was wearing a pale blue gown of some very fine material and on her head was the same hat with feathers and a bird such as I'd never seen before.

"It's them!" I shouted excitedly, clutching at Roddie's arm. "The castle folk."

Then I saw his face set in grim lines.

"Why, what's the matter, Roddie?" I said, alarmed.

He turned to me impatiently. "Do you not see?" he said. "They're heading straight for the island."

Only then did it dawn on me. "The current!" I said. "They'll be caught in it."

"Aye," he said seriously. "And they'll be drowned if we don't turn them back. Now, shout for all you're worth, Kirsty!"

But it did no good. They heard us all right. Sound carries well over water and they were only about fifteen yards away. They just turned and waved, or at least the boy did. And, as he did, I saw a pleasant, friendly face, untroubled because unaware of danger. The girl turned once, then back again with no wave or smile on her face, and though I could not see her eyes for the feathers which drooped forward on her hat, I thought her mouth looked sulky.

"It's no good, Roddie," I said. "They're taking no notice."

"Fools!" he said again. "Come on, Kirsty. If they get caught in that undertow, they won't stand a chance. Just look at how he's handling the oars."

And indeed, even to my inexpert eye, the boy did not seem to be doing too well, lunging at the water with the oars rather than dipping smoothly. Roddie grasped my hand and pulled me down the slope.

"Come on," he said. "We can't just stand here and watch."

Roddie's legs were longer than mine and his feet surer and I felt myself tumble as we ran down on to the sand. I got up, trying to dust the sand from my skirts.

"No time for that, Kirsty," he said. He had already got the boat in the water and he picked me up bodily and set me in it.

"Now take the rope," he said. "And when the time comes, do exacdy as I say."

I looked at him, momentarily amused. As if I could do anything else! Then my amusement vanished as I saw just how dangerous the situation was. I took the rope and coiled it on my lap. He was rowing very fast now, the oars dipping smoothly and the boat running swiftly in the water. Again he made that wide sweep of the island and the other boat came into view. I looked across at the occupants. The sulky look had disappeared from the girl's face and she was berating the boy for his mishandling of the oars.

"Well, really, Richard!" she was saying, and her voice reached us clearly. "I thought you said you knew about boats. Why, we're beginning to go round in circles."

"Charlotte, I did not say that," came the boy's voice, irritated. "I said I had punted about on the river, that's all. You were the one who said I knew how to handle boats."

At that moment Roddie shouted to them and they both turned towards us. The girl's eyes swept over us. It was obvious that she considered it a great impertinence that we should speak to her, let alone shout at her.

"Just two of the natives, Richard," I heard her say in her clear voice.

But the boy was not listening to her. He had begun to take in something of what Roddie was saying and I saw his face whiten in fear. He turned and said a few words to his companion in a low voice, and I saw a quick flush mount in her cheeks followed by a deadly pallor. I thought she was going to faint but she didn't. Instead she did something infinitely more stupid. She tried to stand up and the little boat rocked perilously in the current.

"Sit down and stay still!" roared Roddie but she already had, frightened by the effect of her movement on the boat.

Roddie turned to me. "We'll have to go closer," he said. "Then, when I say, you will throw the rope and hopefully that idiot of a girl will catch it. With luck we'll be able to tow them back, though the way that lad's rowing, I wouldn't be putting any money on it."

His oars dipped easily in the water and I felt a curious pull on the boat.

"Roddie. . ." I said.

"It's only the edge of the current," he said. "Nothing to worry about yet. Just you get ready."

He began to shout instructions to the other boat and I saw the girl nod her understanding. I also saw that Roddie had begun to paddle against the current to keep our boat steady. The boy in the other boat managed to turn with the bow towards us and the girl clambered carefully behind him.

"On the count of three!" shouted Roddie and nodded to me.

I braced myself, hoping that I could throw the rope far enough. On three, I launched it into the air but it fell short, far short, and I saw dismay on the girl's face. Richard, the boy, was struggling to keep their boat steady.

"Let it go," shouted Roddie. "It'll come round again. Then you can start holding it steady halfway round. That'll give us time to get closer."

I felt my lips dry. I could already feel the pull on the boat from the current.

"Roddie. . ." I whispered.

"And would you leave them in their foolishness, Kirsty?" he said. "Don't worry. I'll not bring you to any harm."

I drew the rope in once more and coiled it in my lap again, heavy from the water. It would be harder to throw this time, I thought, as I watched the drops of water mingle with the sand on my skirt and turn to muddy streaks.

"Now!" Roddie shouted and, without thinking, I cast the rope into the air.

Unbelievably, it sailed straight and true, and the girl reached out and caught it. I felt the pull on the boat and saw the rope run through her hands. She flinched then grasped it. The little boat rocked dangerously with her movement but she steadied herself and I saw her tie the rope in what I hoped was a secure knot to the bow. I looked back at Roddie. He was still paddling against the current and I heard him shout to the boy.

"We row together on my call . . . now!"

Then I saw the muscles strain round his mouth and in his neck as he dipped the oars and began to row, shouting each time as his oars cleaved the water. At first we did not move and I looked anxiously at the boy in the other boat. He had not got the rhythm and I felt us being pulled towards them. "Listen, can't you?" I screamed. "I'll count." And I began – "*One!* Two! Three!" – in time to the dipping of Roddie's oars. If nothing else, it would leave him more energy for rowing.

At last I felt our boat resist. Slowly, inch by inch, it made headway and I knew that the boy had found the rhythm at last. I watched Roddie, hardly daring to breathe as his strokes grew swifter and the drag on our stern lessened, and all the time I kept shouting the beat of the oars.

Gradually Roddie's muscles relaxed, his strokes grew smoother, and I felt the boat slip through the water. We were out of danger. But I kept up the chant until I felt our boat grind on the shingle and turned to pull on the rope.

When I turned back, I saw that the look of strain on Roddie's face had been replaced by anger and, no sooner had the other two set foot on land, than he was standing over them, a good head taller than the boy.

"And what do you mean by taking a boat out on water you do not know, when you hardly know how to handle one?" he said.

I saw the boy's face harden for a moment in anger. Then he looked down, seeming to compose himself, and when he looked up again there was only embarrassment in his eyes. The girl's head came up.

"How dare you speak to my cousin like that?" she said. "Don't you know who we are?"

She drew herself up to her full height and I saw her eyes flash blue fire as she looked at Roddie. She was nearly as tall as he was. Her pale blue gown was water-spattered and her hat knocked askew. She pulled it from her head, taking pins and ribbons with it and, as she did so, her hair fell about her shoulders in a cascade of gold. I saw Roddie start, then he said gruffly, "Aye, we know who you are, you're the castle folk."

She laughed. "The castle folk," she said in imitation of his accent and I saw a dull flush creep over his face.

"I am Miss Charlotte Munro," she continued. "And this is my cousin Richard, son of the Laird of Morach."

"I'm afraid the son of the Laird of Morach has been made to look a complete fool," the boy said ruefully.

I saw a spark fly between him and Roddie. The son of the Laird of Morach was indeed very angry, despite his manner.

Then Roddie said smoothly, "Not at all. You didn't know about the current."

"True," said the boy. "But, all the same, you probably saved our lives."

The girl turned to him. "That, Richard, is no reason for this boy to address us in the way he has. He is no doubt one of your tenants." She turned again to Roddie. "I suppose you will want a reward," she said. "You may come up to the castle tomorrow. You will find the Laird not ungrateful."

A muscle twitched in Roddie's cheek but he said very quiedy, "For the son of the Laird, no man in Morach would have done less. There is no need of thanks – or reward."

I saw the bright flush mount her cheeks as the insult found its mark, then she turned on her heel and marched away.

The boy turned to us, clearly torn between the need to apologize for his cousin's behaviour and the difficulty of doing so.

Roddie forestalled him. "We bid you welcome to Morach," he said, offering his hand.

The Laird's son took it in his own and smiled. "It's a sorry impression I've made my first day here," he said.

I warmed to him for his use of the idiom of the glen, not as his cousin had used it, but as a natural expression of friendship. Then that clear, high voice came again and he grimaced.

"You'd better be going," I said, and he pulled a face.

"I'll get merry hell from her for this," he said, lapsing back into his own way of speech. "We'll meet again."

"Morach is not a big place," I said and he smiled before hurrying off over the shingle.

"The boy's nice," I said, turning to Roddie.

"The boy was as mad as a wet hen for having to be rescued," said Roddie. "And he'll hold it against me. But at least he knew enough not to say thank you."

"The girl is impossible," I said. "She made me feel like a tinker."

He laughed. "The natives, she called us. Aye, she's a fine one. Did you see the spark in those eyes and the colour of her hair? My, but it was bonny!"

I turned on him in disgust. "Roddie MacLelland," I said, "you're surely not going to let a pretty face and yellow hair blind you to such rudeness?"

"Ach," he said, "she had a fine fire in her and did you not see that she was hurt? Her hands were bleeding from handling that rope."

I paused. "I hadn't noticed," I said. "But that doesn't excuse her!" I shouted after him as he moved away.

He turned, his face bright with amusement.

"Away with you, Kirsty Strachan!" he said. "You're just jealous because your hair is as dark as the raven's wing. And hers isn't yellow," he shouted back as he reached the lych-gate. "It's golden. Now get on home and I don't know what you're going to tell your mother for you look a sorry sight."

Then he was gone. I stamped my foot in vexation and began to make my way home. With any luck my mother would still be up at the castle. Golden indeed! I thought. Who would ever have guessed Roddie MacLelland could be so poetic? And I wasn't jealous, or so I told myself.

That was the first time the four of us came together, Charlotte, Richard, Roddie and I, and set in motion a pattern that was to grow more complex as the years went on, and rock Morach on its heels with a scandal that had its roots in the past.

Chapter 3

Next day I was summoned to the castle. A note was brought by hand very early simply requesting my mother to bring me with her and giving no further explanation. Mother was dismayed.

"What can it mean, Kirsty?" she said. "What have you done?"

My lips were dry. Not from fear of telling her what could be the only reason for my summons, but because I knew she would be angry at my association with Roddie. I began to explain haltingly. It was almost comical to watch her, torn between gratification at my part in the rescue and consternation at my having been out in a boat with Roddie MacLelland to Druid Island. So I was alternately scolded and praised as she shook out my Sunday clothes and polished my only pair of good shoes. The scoldings continued as she hurried me up the glen to the castle but were soon replaced by curiosity as to what the "young lady" had been wearing and how the Laird's son had seemed.

I felt my steps dragging as we approached the great gates. I had never been inside the castle, not even with Father, and I was at the same time excited by the prospect and terrified of it. Beyond the enormous ornamental gates, the carriage drive swept in a wide curve round a broad lawn to the front of the castle. It stood high on a ballustraded terrace, the twin towers throwing back the morning sunlight in diamonds of brightness. Close to, it was even bigger than I had imagined and, to my astonishment and my mother's confusion, the great doors were thrown back as we approached. Instead of making our way round to the back as Mother had intended, we were forced to mount the broad steps to the main entrance.

A man stood there, tall and dark and dressed in worn tweeds, and I heard my mother say softly, "Heavens above, Kirsty! It's the Laird himself." And she bobbed a curtsey, pulling on my hand to do the same.

But I was looking into a face so full of warmth and welcome that instead I found myself putting out my hand to him. I heard my mother's scandalized gasp as I repeated the words Roddie had used to his son.

"I bid you welcome to Morach," I said.

He took my hand in both his own and drew me towards him.

"So you are Jamie Strachan's daughter," he said.

I smiled in pleasure. "You knew my father?"

"The best ghillie in Scotland," he replied and, turning to my mother, added, "We had some fine times together when I was a boy, Mrs Strachan. I would like to have seen him again."

I looked at him curiously. There was a note of real sadness in his voice – a voice, I noticed, that still had something of Highland softness in it.

Mother curtseyed again and muttered her thanks, but he would have none of it.

"It is I who owe the thanks," he said. "But for your daughter and her young friend, my son and my niece could have got themselves killed."

He led us into the great hall and I marvelled at the magnificence of the fine, two-branched, oak staircase and the portraits which covered the panelled walls. On a huge circular table which stood in the centre of the hall, was a bowl of the most beautiful flowers I had ever seen. I could not even name them, for at that time I knew nothing of flowers unless they were wild. I found myself staring at them in wonder – gawping, I suppose Roddie would say.

Then I heard the Laird say to my mother, "You will take a cup of tea with me,

Mrs Strachan?" From her face, I could see that she would rather have refused, but I also saw that behind the Laird's kindliness there was an authority that she could not but bow to. He turned to me.

"Kirsty," he said, "you will find my niece and my son in the garden. I think they will have something to say to you."

As if by magic, young Effie, the housekeeper's daughter, appeared at my elbow and I watched as Mother was led away in some confusion by the Laird. Once they were out of sight, Effie linked her arm in mine.

"Such a stramash last night, Kirsty," she said with relish. "You've never seen the like before! I'm sure the whole house heard it – with the Laird shouting at the young Miss and the young Master trying to get his twopence worth in. And at the end of it, all he could get out of them was that the girl was called Kirsty, for they'd heard the laddie say your name. And we were sent for and I said there was only one Kirsty in Morach that fitted the description and it was you, was it not?"

I laughed as I followed Effie down a corridor towards the back of the house. Effie had always been the same. She could talk the hind legs off a donkey, the Dominie would say. And she was always getting into trouble for it when she should have been working.

He hadn't made any objections when she left the school earlier than she should have done to come up to the castle to help her mother.

"Yes, it was me," I said, but she was off again.

"And it was Roddie MacLelland that was with you, was it not? Oh, we were sure it had to be and there's not so many boats in the village that you could make a mistake. Aye, we thought it had to be Roddie and he was sent for this morning though he's not come yet, if indeed he'll come at all. That Roddie's just a law unto himself. But what we couldn't understand at all, Kirsty, is what you were doing out in a boat to the island with Roddie MacLelland." And she gave me a sly sideways glance.

I opened my mouth to reply but was saved the trouble as another voice cut in.

"She was invited, Effie Robertson, which is more than you'll ever be," said Roddie. "Now give your tongue a rest and take me to the Laird – I've been asked to call," he finished with more than a hint of mockery in his voice.

"Losh, what a fright you gave me!" said Effie, tucking a loose strand of hair back under her cap. "And where did you come from?"

"I've told you, I was invited to call, so I've called," said Roddie.

"And just walked in without a by your leave," she said.

"I came in by the back door," he said. "Wasn't that the proper thing for a peasant to do?"

I glanced at him swiftly, struck by the note in his voice, and saw for the first time the dull flush that suffused his cheeks. Then I looked beyond him to where the dim corridor gave on to the startling light of the gardens and caught a glimpse of the edge of a pale pink gown. I thought I knew what had caused his annoyance – or rather who.

Effie bridled. "I don't know what you're talking about half the time, Roddie MacLelland, or why you can't come into a place like decent folk instead of sneaking in back doors." She drew herself up and I almost laughed at her dignity. "If you'll just come this way, I'll show you where the Laird is," she continued. Then, lapsing into her usual manner to me, "You'll find the pair of young scallywags out there, Kirsty," she said, pointing towards the garden. Then she straightened her cap and marched off.

"This way," she said to Roddie. "And I hope your boots are clean."

I smiled at Roddie as he passed.

"Don't let them intimidate you, Kirsty," he said.

I giggled. "Losh, Roddie MacLelland!" I said in fair imitation of Effie. "I don't even know what the word means."

He smiled back and I breathed a sigh of relief. He had been in no mood to receive thanks from the Laird graciously. Then my hand flew to my mouth as I remembered that my mother was there too. Well, there was nothing I could do about that, I thought, as I stepped out of the dimness and into the garden.

The sun was so bright and the flowers so brilliant that I was dazzled for a moment.

Then a soft voice said, "Miss Strachan," and Richard Munro came forward to meet me.

I said the first thing that came into my head. "You mustn't call me Miss Strachan. Nobody ever does."

"Kirsty then," he smiled. "And you must call me Richard."

I liked the sound of my name as he said it. He said it as if it were strange to him.

"I must apologize not only for putting you into danger on the loch yesterday but also for the haste in which I left without thanking you properly," he went on. "I was rather concerned for my cousin's welfare," and his eyes moved beyond me.

"Oh, for goodness' sake, Richard, don't make such a meal of it!" Charlotte Munro said impatiendy.

She was wearing a gown of palest pink. Tiny rosebuds were pinned to a satin ribbon of deeper pink which encircled her impossibly small waist and on her head she wore a wide straw hat which framed her face charmingly. She moved towards me.

"Well, Kirsty," she said and it was said as one would speak a servant's name. "It would seem that I too have to thank you."

She did not hold out her hand, but that may have been because it was injured, I thought, taking note of the bandage.

"I hope your hand is not giving you pain," I said.

She looked at it impatiently. "It's nothing," she said. "Just a rope burn. The boy put some sort of dressing on it."

I felt my eyes widen in astonishment.

"Roddie?" I said.

"I believe that's what he calls himself," she said. "It's a strange sort of name."

"It's short for Roderick," I said absent-mindedly, still too surprised to think how to ask the questions I wanted to ask.

Richard came to my rescue. "He was very kind," he said. "He came up to the house last night to enquire after Charlotte's hand and brought some salve of his grandmother's making. I'm afraid Charlotte rather offended him again this morning."

She turned on him. "I merely said that these peasant remedies were often remarkably effective."

Richard coughed. "It didn't go down too well, I'm afraid," he said.

I was staring at Charlotte in amazement. "I can imagine," I said. "His grandmother is very clever with herbal remedies. With no doctor nearer than Fort William, the village depends on her a great deal."

Richard had gone bright red. "So I understand," he said.

I waited. There was clearly something else.

"Oh, for goodness' sake!" broke in Charlotte. "If you must know, I only asked him if his grandmother was a witch. There's no need to get all hot and bothered about it."

I think I would have said something to her then, but Effie appeared at my shoulder.

"The Laird wants to see you, Kirsty," she said, bobbing a curtsey in the vague direction of Charlotte and Richard.

"I'll come now, Effie," I said and, as I turned to go, I heard Charlotte say almost pathetically to her cousin, "Really, Richard, these servants have a very odd manner. They aren't exactly disrespectful but. . ."

The rest was lost to me as I followed Effie back down the narrow corridor, with her chattering all the way. But I smiled to myself as I thought that it would take Miss Charlotte Munro a long time to accustom herself to, much less understand, the relationship that existed between a Highland laird and his tenants.

Effie continued to chatter until we reached a door which led off the great hall, then she propelled me through it, popped her head round with an "It's Kirsty, Laird!" and disappeared.

I found myself in a room of great beauty. Long windows hung with brocade curtains looked out on to a sunny lawn and everywhere were vases and figurines in what I learned later was Chinese porcelain of great value. My mother sat on the edge of a delicately embroidered sofa, presiding uncomfortably over a tray of silver tea things. In a corner, his back to the window so that his face was shadowed, stood Roddie, holding his china cup and saucer so grimly I wondered it did not shatter. The Laird rose to greet me and motioned Mother to pour me out a cup of tea.

"Now, Kirsty," he said as he setded me beside my mother. "Your mother and I have had a talk and I have made a suggestion to her that she seems to think well of. I hope you will listen carefully to what I have to say and give me an honest answer."

I took the cup from Mother, marvelling at its fragility, my mind in a turmoil wondering what was coming next. He was speaking again.

"Charlotte has been in my care for nearly a year now," he said. "Her parents – my sister and her husband – were killed in a tragic accident abroad. It has not been an easy time for her, for she was their only child and they doted on her. My decision to come back to Morach after my own wife's death was not made lightly. Nor, I admit, was it made any easier by having to take Charlotte so far away from what she has always been used to. But Richard will one day inherit this estate and it is only right that he should live here and know the people, that he should be prepared for the running of it when the time comes." He paused for a moment, then said, "Besides, I had a great desire to return myself."

He placed his cup and saucer on the table and turned to me. "What I did not realize was how lonely it might be for Charlotte. Richard will be away for a good part of the year and we are rather remote here at Morach. She is accustomed to more lively company than she will find here. The parties and outings she was used to helped to take her mind off the loss she has suffered. What I am about to say now is merely a suggestion and I would wish you to consider it carefully before you answer."

I looked enquiringly towards my mother, but her head was bent and I could not catch her eye.

"Kirsty," the Laird continued, "you have shown yourself both courageous and level-headed. I want you to come to Blair Morach as companion to Charlotte. You will, of course, share Charlotte's governess, but you have before you another choice which, I understand, you know nothing about." He looked at Mother and she nodded, though I thought I saw apprehension in her eyes. He went on. "The Dominie has expressed himself willing to take you for extra studies so that you may be able to apply for a place next year to train as a teacher and, in gratitude for what you have done, I should be glad to pay for your training. The choice is yours, Kirsty. Think carefully before you answer and follow your heart, my dear."

It was only his last words that stopped me from crying out in delight. I held my tongue and looked at my mother. Her head was bent and I could not see her face, but I knew as surely as if she had shouted the words aloud what she wished me to do. Had she not always told me I was different, wanted me to be a lady? And yet she had no need to tell the Laird of what the Dominie had said, no need ever to tell even me.

I wanted to say no. To be companion to that spoiled brat of a girl, to be treated as a servant by her, to come here instead of following my ambition! He had said "follow your heart". I looked instinctively towards Roddie but his face was deep in shadow, the light behind him. Though I could not see his face, I fancied I could imagine the look on it and the thoughts behind it and I turned towards the Laird to give my answer.

Then, as I did so, I saw my mother's face, anxious, eager. I looked into her eyes. My glance rested on her hands as they lay on her lap, the delicate china held within them and I saw their roughness and the thousand little pinpricks that came of sewing far into the night by the light of an inadequate lamp. She wanted the best for me. She had done her best for me, Could I not do this for her?

As I turned to the Laird and said, "I shall be pleased to come as companion to your niece," I heard two things.

On my left my mother gasped with pleasure and relief so that the cup tinkled in the saucer whilst on my right there was a stifled oath and Roddie's cup went down on a small table with a crash that nearly shattered it. The Laird barely had time to smile his thanks before Roddie was amongst us.

"I'll say good day then, Laird," he said.

They stood facing each other, Roddie nearly as tall as his host, and, but for the clothes, it would have been hard to tell which was the laird and which the tenant.

"I'm sorry you feel you cannot accept my help in recompense for saving my son and my niece from certain death," said the Laird.

Roddie gave him a level look. "I'll say to you what I said to your son," he replied. "No man in Morach would have done less." His mouth curved in a grim little smile. "There is no need of recompense," he said. "You have been away from Morach a long time indeed to think that there is. And each man must make his own way."

I looked at him then, barely more than a boy. But I got no answering look from him.

"Good day, Mrs Strachan, Miss Strachan," he said, and to me his voice was heavy with mockery. Then he was gone from the room.

Chapter 4

And so began my life at the castle. It was a strange kind of life, going up there each morning with Mother and parting with her as she made her way to the sewing room in the servants' quarters and I took myself upstairs to the schoolroom to wait for Charlotte and her governess.

The governess was a small woman with a pronounced French accent and seemed more concerned with my manners and clothes than with my education. As for Charlotte, she would avoid lessons if she could and led poor Mademoiselle Lallande through hoops to put off the moment when the books would be opened and we would settle down to work.

Sometimes I longed for the village school and the sombre, wise old Dominie who had taught us there but, each time I did, I felt guilty. Mother was so pleased, so delighted that I was being given the chance to become a lady.

I never enlightened her as to Charlotte's attitude to that. To her I was a paid companion and treated as such, and if Mademoiselle

Lallande had any sympathy for my position then it was because my situation was not unlike hers. Effie, on the other hand, had no sympathy for my situation. She had made it quite clear that she resented my presence at the castle.

But I got on well with Mademoiselle Lallande despite her cries of horror at what she called my "barbaric ways", and I learned which spoons and forks to use at which meal and, instead of sprawling on chairs, I sat neatly, my feet tucked in and my hands in my lap.

One thing I did have Charlotte to thank for was my new clothes. I had been going up to the castle for several weeks when she said across the schoolroom table, "Mademoiselle Lallande, I really cannot bear to sit here looking at her any longer. We really must do something about those clothes."

Mademoiselle Lallande looked at me sympathetically.

"And what does the little one feel?" she said.

I smiled. She quite often called me "the little one" though I was already half a head taller than her.

"They are the best I have," I said simply, thinking of the long hours mother had sat sewing the skirt I was wearing and hemming the tucks of the white blouse. She had gone specially to Fort William in MacCrimmon's trap to get such fine cotton and, I suspected, used the last of our savings in doing so.

Charlotte lost patience. "It really is too bad. You sit there like a mouse in your servant's clothes, studying your books and trying to make me feel guilty. I won't have it!"

I tried to remonstrate with her. "I'm quite happy with my clothes," I said. "And I like learning."

She jumped up from the table and stamped her foot. "There you go again, Miss Goody Two Shoes!" she said. "I won't have it. Come with me." And she swept from the room, her fine white lawn gown fluttering.

I smiled apologetically at Mademoiselle Lallande, who raised her hands in an expressive gesture.

"You had better go, my child," she said. "When she has made up her mind to have her own way, then have it she will."

Charlotte was halfway down the staircase as I emerged from the schoolroom.

"Oh, come along, mouse," she said and I hurried after her.

I hadn't been in her bedroom before and, for all the splendour I'd become used to at Blair Morach, I gasped as I entered. Effie was there, arranging brushes on the dressing-table. She looked sideways at me and smiled knowingly.

"Your mouth is hanging open," she said and I closed it with a snap.

It was not the room's size that took my breath away but the richness and delicacy of its furnishings. I know now the names of the things it contained – that the bed was a half-tester canopied in palest pink silk, that the rugs on the polished floor were Chinese and the delicate furnishings, French. Light flooded the room from the two long windows where silk brocade curtains the exact colour of the bed hangings stirred gently in the breeze, and I thought I had never seen a room so lovely.

"Don't just stand there," said Charlotte crossly, as she disappeared through a small door to my right.

Effie adjusted the angle of a brush. "Hurry, now, Kirsty," she said. "The young mistress likes her servants to jump when she snaps her fingers."

I didn't answer her, but followed Charlotte into the dressing-room and watched in awe as she flung open the doors of a great armoire and began to cast clothes from it.

"These you may have," she said, frowning as she chose from the rail of gowns. "They're either too small for me or I've grown tired of them."

I looked in wonder at the growing pile of silks and satins, merinos and serges. Then

45

hats and pelisses began to appear. Effie stood in the doorway, her eyes fixed hungrily on the pretty clothes.

"Stop!" I said in confusion. "I can't wear these."

Charlotte turned and looked at me in my plain grey skirt and white blouse.

"Why not?" she said. "Look what you're wearing now."

"She's wearing servant's clothes," said Effie sourly. "You mustn't give her ideas above her station."

"It isn't that," I said, angered. "But these clothes suit me. How can I wear such finery as this in the village?"

I saw understanding dawn. "Oh," she said. "I didn't think."

I wondered then if Charlotte was less cruel than she was thoughtless and, oddly enough, I felt quite sorry for her at that moment.

"Look," I said, picking up a soft merino in a deep wine colour. "I'll have this. It's quite plain."

"Yes," she said. "It never suited me."

I smiled. "And here," I went on, "I can wear this one."

It was a printed cotton in lilac with a pretty pattern of tiny flowers. She looked at me in wonder.

"And what about these?" she said, one daintily-shod foot kicking at the pile of silks and satins.

I shook my head. "These will be enough," I said firmly.

She looked puzzled. "What a strange creature you are, Kirsty," she said. "Don't you like clothes?"

My eyes rested on the pile of lovely things in front of me and I wanted to say – Yes, I love clothes and I want to wear these things but my mother is a servant in your house and I am your paid companion. But I didn't and, at her next words, I was glad I hadn't. She wouldn't have understood.

"No doubt your mother will be able to alter them," she said. "Send the maid down with them."

I saw Effie's mouth tighten and I was angry with Charlotte. I bent and folded the clothes neatly before saying, "I shall take them home with me this evening."

"As you wish," she said. Then, "Oh, do leave that for Effie to do. You aren't a servant, Kirsty." And she swept out of the room.

"That's the trouble, isn't it?" said Effie. "If you aren't a servant, what are you, Kirsty?"

There was no sympathy in her eyes, only hostility.

"Does she treat you badly?" I asked.

Effie put her head on one side. "I have ways of getting my own back," she said. "Servants do, you know."

I looked at her. I was sure she did get her own back.

I gathered up the gowns and walked towards the door.

"There now," said Effie. "You'll look a treat for Master Richard and I don't suppose for a minute he'll recognize those hand-me-downs."

I kept on walking.

Summer was almost gone when I found I had a free morning for once. Charlotte was going to Fort William to shop and had said to me casually, "I shall take Mademoiselle Lallande, since you have no liking for clothes."

I bit my tongue, determined not to say that I should have loved a trip to Fort William to the big shops.

"You needn't come up until after lunch," she said. "No doubt you'll bury your nose in a book all morning."

If she hadn't added that last remark I probably would have "buried my nose in a book". Instead, I decided to walk down to the churchyard.

I tidied the cottage and set off. There wasn't much to be done at home now, for Mother and I took our main meals at the castle and, with the extra money coming in, there wasn't the never-ending pile of mending to be done.

The day was calm and clear as I slipped through the lych-gate and I felt a rising of spirits I had not known for a long time. When I saw him bending over his little boat, I said with real pleasure, "Roddie, how nice to see you!"

He turned and his face lit with a sudden involuntary smile before the shutters came down and his eyes took in my gown and neat black-buttoned boots.

I was wearing the wine-coloured merino for which Mother had crocheted a fine white lace collar and my hair, which until this summer I had been used to wear tied back with a ribbon or neatly plaited, was twisted in a heavy knot at the nape of my neck. When I had looked into the old spotted mirror this morning I'd thought I was almost pretty, my hair darker than ever against the glowing colour of the gown.

"My, Kirsty, they're making a fine lady of you up there!"

I felt quick tears sting the back of my eyes. I had not seen him for weeks and all he could do was mock me.

"It's more than can be said for you, Roddie MacLelland," I said, looking at his worn clothes. "Why, you're not even wearing boots."

His feet were bare and brown as he stood at the water's edge. "And why would I be wearing boots when the earth is soft beneath my feet and I'm in and out of the water with the boat?"

I looked down at my own neatly shod feet and felt an unreasonable anger and a desire to tear off my boots and run barefoot as I had done every summer until now. Instead I said primly, "And how is the boat?"

"She's fine," he said, but my eye had caught the beginning of the name he was carefully painting on the side and I felt hurt twist sharply in me.

"*The Raven. . .,*" I said. "I thought you were going to call it *The Friendship.*"

He didn't look at me as he said, "Ah well, friendship has a habit of melting away."

I took a step towards him and reached out a hand to touch his arm. "Roddie," I said to the dark head bent over the boat, "why are you being like this? Why do you have such anger towards me?"

He wiped his hands on a rag as he turned to face me. "It's your own business," he said, "and none of mine. But I thought you had ambition like me. I thought you had more in you than to throw yourself away playing nursemaid to a spoilt slip of a girl."

I found myself shaking his arm in vexation. "That's not fair, Roddie, and you know it. Why, you wouldn't believe the change in Mother since I've gone up to the castle. She's so well now, and happy."

He put his hand briefly on mine. "So that's it," he said. "I'm sorry, Kirsty. I thought—"

"You thought I liked the luxury of life up there," I said. "Well, it might interest you to know that I don't. I'd rather be off after the summer to train as a teacher but where's the money to come from for that?" Then my hand flew to my mouth. "Roddie, your scholarship!"

"It's all settled," he said. "I go to Edinburgh next week."

I clapped my hands in delight. "But that's wonderful!" I said. "The Dominie will be pleased. What did he say?"

His face was bright with laughter. "He said, 'Aye, ye've done no' sae bad, Roddie, but doan't let it gang tae yer heid.' "

I laughed with him. "And your grandmother, Roddie?"

"She'll be all right till I can provide for her," he said. "She's got a wee bit put by and there's always her medicines. I'll be working on the estate in the holidays and that'll bring in something."

I looked at him in astonishment. "On the estate?" I said. "And you've the cheek to lecture me about being up at the castle!"

He turned back to his painting. "An honest day's work for an honest day's pay," he said.

"I'll not be putting up with some pert miss and her tantrums for my money."

A new thought struck me. "She shouldn't have said what she did about your grandmother," I said.

"Ach, she's just a silly lassie that says the first thing that comes into her head!" he said. "She needs taking in hand, that's all."

"You're very charitable," I said. "It's not like you."

He grinned wickedly. "Aye well, she's a very bonny lass," he said.

"Oh, you're impossible!" I said, laughing. "Can you not be serious? I'll miss you when you go to Edinburgh and, with Richard off to Oxford, it'll be dull up there."

His hand came out and gripped mine almost fiercely for a moment as he said, "I can be serious about this, Kirsty. Don't let your head be turned up there at the castle. They may be the Munros of Morach, the Loch and our folk, but they're different for all that. Just remember, Kirsty, you're better sticking to your own kind."

I felt myself blushing furiously as he let me go. "I must get back," I said. "She'll be home soon."

It was stretching the truth for I knew Charlotte would be gone for the better part of the day, but I had to get away. I started back up the path but his voice stopped me.

"Did you see the name on the boat?" he said.

I looked. He had finished it now. The paint was still wet and the words shimmered in the sun – *The Raven's Wing*.

"Oh, Roddie!" I said, feeling suddenly miserable.

"You've got bonny hair," he said, "and a sensible head under it. Just keep it that way."

I fled up the path, unable to meet his eyes.

If I have avoided any mention of Richard in the weeks I had been at Blair Morach, it is not because he wasn't there, but because I hardly knew what to think of my own feelings. As I made my way up the glen, I tried to face them for once. He was so different from the village boys. In that Roddie was perfecdy right. But the difference lay in things other than wealth and position. He was gentle and kind to me. I expect Roddie would put that down to never having wanted for anything but, to be fair, Charlotte had never wanted for anything either, she could not be called gentle and her kindness was tinged with patronage.

My pleasure in the beauty of the day was gone as I wondered whether there had been more to Roddie's words than merely a warning to a poor girl suddenly catapulted into a world of plenty. How could he know of my feelings for Richard when I barely knew myself?

Then the picture of Effie with her sly and knowing smiles rose before me. Had I been stupid to think I could hide from her the way Richard affected me? It was just the kind of thing she would notice and if she had voiced her thoughts to Roddie, who else would she have gossiped to? Oh, it was too bad! I thought. That's what comes of living in a little place like Morach where people are constantly under each other's eye, their every action talked about. For the first time in my life I almost hated my lovely Morach.

Then common sense reasserted itself. Roddie's words had not meant any more than they said. After all, there was no harm in liking Richard and that was all it was. I was barely seventeen and there was no sense in worrying myself over such an attraction. It was perfectly natural.

And besides, there was an underlying rivalry between Roddie and Richard. They had never really got on. Richard still resented the fact that Roddie had rescued him. I could see it in the way he sometimes looked at Roddie, as if the incident still rankled. And Roddie was very conscious that Richard was the Laird's son. It made him wary of Richard. His warnings probably had more to do with how he felt about Richard than how I felt about the young laird.

I felt quite cheered as I made my way to the castle library and was looking forward to an hour or two's pleasant reading. But as I entered I caught a glimpse of a blond head bending over a book. He was sitting in the window seat and I would have withdrawn had he not looked up at that moment and said, his face brightening with pleasure, "Why, Kirsty, what a welcome sight you are! Come and talk to me for, I confess, I'm bored beyond belief."

And, closing his book with a snap, Richard came forward to meet me.

Chapter 5

"Richard!" I said. "I thought you were going to Fort William with Charlotte."

"What?" he said, laughing. "To trail around after her and carry her parcels? Not me." He gestured towards the library shelves which stretched from floor to ceiling. "I've been examining the library, and what a magnificent one it is! Did you know what a lot of books there are on the history of Scotland here?"

I laughed. "Oh, we're very proud of our history, we Scots," I said.

He looked hurt. "Don't say 'we Scots' like that," he said. "After all, I'm half Scottish myself."

"Oh, I didn't mean . . . I'm sorry," I began but he interrupted me, laughing.

"Now I've upset you," he said. "I was only joking. Come and look at the book I found. It's fascinating."

I smiled up at him as he drew me into the room. "I thought you were bored beyond belief," I said.

"An exaggeration," he replied. "Not that I wouldn't rather talk to you than read dusty old tomes."

My heart gave a little skip but he was holding the book out to me. I looked at the worn lettering on the cheap cloth cover. That for one thing was unusual. Most of the books were beautifully bound in leather and decorated with ornate gold tooling. I read the title curiously. It was in old-fashioned script.

"*Heathen Practices in the Lands of Morach and the Cults Associated With the Druid Island*," I said. "Good heavens! What on earth is in it?"

He took it from me again. "All sorts of strange rites and witchcraft," he said, rolling his eyes dramatically, and I laughed. "Perhaps I'd better not show it to you after all. It might corrupt you."

"Oh, let me see," I said. "Roddie was talking about a book like this. Maybe it's the same one."

I reached for the book. But he put it behind his back, teasing me.

"No, no, it isn't fit for the eyes of a young lady," he said. "Roddie should never have spoken to you of such things."

"Oh, come on, Richard," I protested. "Now you've made me more curious than ever." And I reached again for the book.

It was thoughtless of me, I suppose, but I was still surprised when his arm went round me and he held me to him. I looked up, not yet understanding, and his mouth came down on mine. For a moment I could do nothing as I savoured the strangeness of my first kiss, then I came to myself and wriggled free. He made no attempt to stop me, merely looked at me ruefully, his head on one side.

"Sorry, Kirsty," he said, "but you really must learn not to look at a man like that. It's too tempting."

"Like what?" I said, torn between confusion and indignation.

"Oh, eager and fresh and sparkling," he said; then with a twinkle, "Do you want me to go on?"

"No," I said, turning away from him. "Please don't."

I heard his step as he came towards me and his voice low as he said, "Kirsty..."

Then the door swung open and the Laird came in.

"Ah, Kirsty," he said, "I see you've been entertaining this young scapegrace."

Richard laughed and came to stand beside me, looking down and forcing me to look away.

"Indeed she has," he said.

The Laird noticed nothing.

"I came to look for some books I'm sure are here somewhere," he said, looking round vaguely.

I saw Richard slip his own little book into his pocket as he said, "Well, I've been pottering about here all morning. Perhaps I can help."

The Laird looked at him in surprise. "Indeed?" he said. "Kirsty is certainly having a good effect on you then. I've never known you willingly read a book in your life."

"Oh Father," said Richard, an edge of irritation in his voice, "don't be such a bore. After all, the leopard does sometimes change its spots and, besides, I'll get enough of books at Oxford soon."

"Humph!" said the Laird. "I'll believe it when I see it. And as for Oxford, it's as well known for the scrapes young men get into as the learning they acquire."

I saw a spark flare momentarily behind Richard's eyes but he said mildly enough, "What were you looking for?"

"Some books on the law," said his father. "I wanted to let Roddie see them."

"Roddie?" I said.

"Yes," he said. "He's an interesting boy, your young friend, Kirsty. I understand he's going off to university in Edinburgh soon. Wants to be a lawyer. I offered him the job as ghillie here," he went on. "He's young for it, of course, but he's been trained by your father and there's no better recommendation than that as far as I can see. Besides, I've heard good accounts of him. But he looked me straight in the eye. 'I appreciate the offer,' he said, 'but I've other plans,' and then he went on to tell me about this lawyer business. I admit I was surprised, though I ought not to have been. The parish schools have a fine reputation for sending their young men off to university." He sighed. "There's a lot I've forgotten in my years away from Morach."

My sympathy went out to him then as I felt the weight of his sadness and I glanced across at Richard. He was looking out of the long window, down the glen to the loch, and his face had a grim set to it. I could not guess at the thoughts behind it. The Laird was speaking again.

"I've persuaded Roddie to come up to Blair Morach during his vacations," he said. "He's agreed to take Richard on, show him what estate work at Morach really involves." He turned to his son and his voice was anxious as he said, "You'd like that, Richard. After all, it'll be yours some day and there's no better way of learning than with a lad of your own age who knows the hills and the glen like the back of his hand."

"Of course, sir," Richard said and his father relaxed.

"It's the way I learned, Kirsty," he said, turning to me, "with your father to teach me," and a shadow passed across his face. It was gone in an instant.

But I did not care to pursue the subject. I had seen Richard's lips tighten at the mention of learning from Roddie. The Laird had clearly not noticed the tension between the two of them. This plan would not help.

"The books, Laird," I said.

"The books," he repeated. "That's what I came for."

Richard found them at last on one of the highest shelves. He needed the tall ladder that ran on rollers round the shelves to reach them. Richard handed them down and I dusted them. They were large, heavy volumes. I wondered at the contradiction as I pictured Roddie bent over musty books like this, the same Roddie who loved the hills and loch and the freedom of open spaces so much. I was just reaching up to take the last book from Richard when he bent towards me.

"Stay," he whispered. "I want to talk to you."

But I didn't want to talk to him, not until I'd had time to think about that kiss and how I had almost responded to it. I turned to the Laird, picking up three of the lighter books.

"I'll take these to Roddie," I said. "I know where he is."

"I'll walk with you to the gates," said the Laird.

I carefully didn't look at Richard as we left, but I heard the amusement in his voice as he said: "That's the nice thing about Morach. It's never very difficult to find anybody."

The Laird was silent as we walked down the drive and I was happy enough to have it that way, for I was busy with my own thoughts. But as we reached the gates he turned and laid a hand on my shoulder.

"We must have a talk about your father one of these days, Kirsty," he said. "I find that coming back to Morach has brought a lot of memories with it. I must be getting old."

I made to protest but he would have none of it. "He was a good man," he said, "a good man." And the shadow was there again on his face as he said it.

I watched him for a moment as he walked back up the drive, looking strangely small against the towering bulk of Blair Morach. Then I felt the weight of the books in my arms and turned my steps towards the churchyard, thinking how pleased Roddie would be. I found him just coming out of the church gate on to the road and he *was* pleased. His face lit up as he turned the pages and I noticed that he handled the books as reverendy as he would a plover's egg found in its delicate nest on the hill.

"Why, this is wonderful, Kirsty! It means I can make a start right away."

I laughed at him. "With any luck you won't have to go to the university at all," I said. "You'll just learn all you need to know from these books and march down to Edinburgh to demand your degree."

He had the grace to look a little shame-faced. "Ah now, Kirsty, don't mock me," he said, "poor scholar that I am."

"What a charlatan!" I said. "And anyway, I gather you won't have much time for study during your holidays."

"You've heard, have you?" he said thoughtfully.

"You might have told me what your 'honest day's work' was," I said. I hesitated. "I think Richard resents it."

He nodded, his eyes serious. "Don't worry," he said. "I'll be careful."

"Of Richard's feelings?" I asked.

"Oh, those as well," he said. Then, before I could ask him what he meant, he grinned. "I'd say of the two of us, I've got the easier job. Young Richard will find himself doing an honest day's work no matter how much he resents it."

"Young Richard!" I said. "Isn't he older than you?"

"No, younger by almost a year," Roddie said and at that moment I felt quite sorry for Richard. I could imagine that his idea of a day's work was far removed from Roddie's.

There was the sound of wheels on the road and we turned as the castle carriage drew up, spurting dust. One look at Charlotte's face as she lowered the window and leaned out told me all I needed to know. The shopping trip had not been a success.

"Big shops, you said, Kirsty," she began, without so much as a greeting. "Have you seen them? How am I expected to put up with it? I shall be a scarecrow before the year is out. And why aren't you at the castle?"

I was trying to think of something to say to mollify her when I heard Roddie's voice say coolly and with the accent grossly exaggerated, "Ach now, Miss Charlotte! You did not expect to find the great and wonderful shops that you are used to in London? We are but poor and simple folk and Fort William seems a wonderfully cosmopolitan place to us."

She looked at him scathingly, unsure whether he was making fun of her.

"I've no doubt for a country yokel it does," she said; then, catching sight of the books, "What have you there?"

I interrupted. "Your uncle has kindly loaned Roddie some books that will help with his studies," I said.

"Studies?" she said, her voice heavy with sarcasm as she looked him over from the top of his unruly head to his bare brown feet. "You? Why, look at you! It's boots you need, not books. Now get in, Kirsty, do! I want to talk to you."

She had shifted her glance from Roddie to me as she said it, so she didn't see the colour drain from his face or the bleakness that had come into his eyes that was the mark of cold fury. The books struck the side of the carriage with such force that, solid as it was, it rocked slightly with the impact. She turned, her hands flying for protection to her face as she looked in horror at Roddie.

What she saw in his eyes made her flinch as he said, "There are your books and much good may they do you, you ill-bred little madam! I suppose you can read? You'll maybe let me know how they compare with the fashion papers. And don't concern yourself. I'll not be touching anything of yours again until you ask me to – nicely."

Her face had flushed an angry and unbecoming red as she gasped for words.

"How dare you!" she screamed. "How dare you speak to me like that! My uncle shall hear of it. I have never been subjected to such an affront."

She was close to tears, though more from anger than from distress, I thought.

Roddie smiled pleasandy up at her, once more in command of himself.

"Aye well, maybe if you had you'd be the possessor of a sight better manners than you are," he said. "And while you're at it, you can tell the Laird that if he wants me to take you on as well as your cousin then he only has to ask. I'd be quite willing to try and make a lady out of you, though I admit it would not be an easy job. Still," he said consideringly, "I like a challenge."

She was almost speechless with rage as she turned to me. "Get in, Kirsty," she said, and, as I hesitated, "please."

I heard Roddie roar with laughter as I gathered up the now dusty books and got into the carriage.

"See?" he said. "You're learning already."

The coachman's face was a study in subdued mirth as he closed the door behind me and I truly did not know who I was more angry with – Roddie for his stupidity in literally throwing the books he could have used so well back in her face or Charlotte for her crass, insensitive jibes.

Chapter 6

Charlotte stormed up to her room as soon as we reached the castle and it was left to poor Mademoiselle Lallande, who had chattered away bravely, trying to pacify her, to go after her. I was in no mood to play peacemaker. It was, of course, all over the castle within minutes of our arrival and I had three visitors to the schoolroom in quick succession. I had retreated there to be out of the way. Mother was first, her face all concern, afraid that I had somehow had a hand in the incident.

I was still asserting that it had been no business of mine when Effie arrived, bursting with curiosity, her quick little eyes darting from me to Mother, trying to glean more information. I was almost at the end of my patience with them when the door opened once more and Richard strode in. He gave my mother a formal greeting and winked casually at Effie as he settled his long length along the window seat. But his arrival was enough, and Mother and Effie left, still chattering excitedly as they went downstairs. I put my hand to my head. It was beginning to throb.

"Thank you, Richard," I said. "I was about to say something unutterably rude to them."

"Impossible," he said, smiling lazily at me. "You're too much the lady."

"You've heard, I suppose," I said.

He spread his hands. "I should think they've heard at Fort William by now," he replied. "I can see the headlines in the newspaper: *Tenant throws the law at the niece of the Laird of Morach and the Loch*."

I laughed. "Oh, you are good for me!" I said. "I suppose I am getting it out of proportion but it made me so angry to see them behaving so foolishly."

"*Am* I good for you?" he said seriously.

His eyes had lost their bantering look and I felt myself on dangerous ground as I said as lightly as I could, "Of course you are. You make me laugh."

"I know that *you* would be good for me," he said. "You would keep me on the straight and narrow."

"Do you need to be kept on the straight and narrow?" I said flippantly. I was not ready for this.

He looked at me with his charming, rueful smile, holding my gaze. "I'm afraid I do," he said, "sometimes."

I looked away. "Has your father heard?" I said quickly.

This time his laughter rang out. "I'm surprised you can't hear them up here," he said. "There's what you would call a 'stramash' going on in Father's study."

I was immediately alarmed. "Not—"

He interrupted. "No, not Roddie," he said. "That's what you were going to say, wasn't it? No, Father is taking Charlotte to task for her rudeness – and about time too, if you ask me."

I relaxed. Roddie could so easily have been in deep trouble. Even with such provocation, he had no excuse for speaking to Charlotte as he had, much less throwing the books at her. Richard's voice interrupted my thoughts.

"You really care what happens to him, don't you?" he said.

I didn't need to ask who he meant. "Roddie's my friend," I said.

"Is that all?" Richard asked. His eyes were flat, unreadable.

I looked at him in surprise. "Yes, of course," I said. "I've known him all my life."

He rose and came towards me. "And am I your friend, Kirsty?" he said. "Would you be so concerned for me if I were in trouble? If I went off the straight and narrow?"

He was quite serious. I could not be flippant any longer. "I would, Richard," I said. "I'd help you." Then, as he remained silent. "You aren't in trouble, are you?"

"No, Kirsty," he said, turning away. "Not yet, but I may hold you to your promise."

When he turned back, his face was its usual pleasant self, but the memory of his words lingered in my mind as we went downstairs together, talking of other things. For all his light-heartedness, there was a darker side to Richard.

Effie met us on the stairs, her face still aglow with excitement. "Miss Charlotte says will you please come to her room, Kirsty – if it's convenient for you," she said.

I stared at her in disbelief as Richard voiced my thoughts.

"Charlotte said that?" he said. "The devil she did, Effie! Begging your pardon for the language, Kirsty," he finished, and Effie giggled.

"She did," she insisted. " 'If it's convenient for her'. Those were her exact words. I remember them particularly."

Richard hooted. "Coming from Charlotte they're pretty memorable," he said. "Well, you'd better go, Kirsty. Couched though it is in terms of the utmost politeness, you can bet your boots it's still a command."

Effie giggled again, delighted at his words, and I decided not to remonstrate with him for speaking of Charlotte this way in front of the housekeeper's daughter. What was the point? Effie knew everything that went on at Blair Morach anyway. As I went, I heard muttered whisperings and another giggle from Effie. I could not help but think that Richard was a little overfamiliar with her but then he was so good-natured, so unlike Charlotte, and was I so very different from Effie? I was also a village girl.

I found Charlotte sitting before her mirror, trying to repair the ravages of what must have been a positive storm of weeping with a cotton pad soaked in cologne. She turned to me at once.

"Kirsty," she said, "do you think me a spoilt, selfish, discourteous child?"

I almost smiled at her earnestness. My anger melted away and I sat down beside her and said carefully, "I think you are rather thoughtless and perhaps a little insensitive to other people's feelings at times, Charlotte, but I don't think you would deliberately set out to hurt anyone."

She looked at me pitifully and a large tear appeared at the corner of one big, blue eye and rolled down her cheek.

"Doesn't anybody like me?" she said.

She *was* like a child and, just as I would have done with one of the infant class at the village school, I put my arm round her shoulders and patted her comfortingly.

"It's very strange for you here," I said. "It isn't at all what you're used to and, although your uncle has been very kind to you, it isn't like having your own parents. I know. I remember what it was like when my father died and *I* still had my mother. You don't."

She put her head down then and really began to sob.

"I wish . . . my . . . mother . . . was here," she hiccupped.

I went on patting her. It was so easy to forget that she had so recently lost her parents, to see only the hard side of Charlotte. But perhaps that was how she had coped with her grief. People coped in strange ways sometimes.

"You were very close to your mother?" I asked.

She nodded, wiping her tears away. "She was my friend," she said simply and, for a moment, I felt a sharp pang of envy. I had never had that kind of relationship with my own mother. I was immediately ashamed of the thought.

"Your uncle is your friend now," I said. "And Richard."

"Uncle said such terrible things to me," she said. "And Richard has never liked me."

I protested. "Your uncle has only your well-being at heart, Charlotte," I said. "You cannot go through life treading on other people's feelings or you will have no friends at all. And as for Richard, why, of course he likes you! You are cousins."

She sniffed miserably. "Oh, no, he doesn't," she said between sniffs. "When we were little he used to tell me stories about witches and goblins to frighten me and he put frogs in my bed."

I laughed and stood up. Now she really was behaving like an infant. "Oh Charlotte," I said, "all little boys do that. You really are being ridiculously childish. That's a long time ago. He's grown-up now."

Her look was positively mulish as she said, "He hasn't changed. People don't, you know."

"What?" I said, laughing. "Does he still put frogs in your bed?"

"No," she said doggedly. "But he still tells me stories."

I lost patience with her. "Oh, for goodness' sake, Charlotte," I said sharply, "grow up."

Her head came up and I thought for a moment she was going to continue with her nonsense but all she said was, "That's what Uncle said."

"Then do it," I replied, somewhat shortly. "What else did he say?"

She picked up the pad of cotton and began to dab at her face again. "That I've got to apologize to that boy."

"Roddie," I said firmly.

"Roddie," she repeated mutinously.

I relented a little. "He won't make it difficult for you," I said.

She looked at me levelly. "He couldn't make it easy," she replied, lifting her chin. "Would you send Effie to me at once? I really must change out of these clothes. I feel I've been wearing them for a hundred years."

"Yes, ma'am," I said, unable to resist it.

As I closed the door, I caught a flash from the blue eyes. In an odd way I was glad to see Charlotte had not been completely tamed.

I don't know what happened between Roddie and Charlotte later that afternoon. Roddie appeared at the castle and was shown into the Laird's study and, from the set of his face, I don't think he escaped altogether lightly from his part in the incident.

But he was carrying the books he had so unceremoniously hurled at Charlotte as he went into the small drawing-room where she was waiting for him. I offered up a silent prayer that he would not repeat the offence. It was some little time before they emerged, Charlotte rather pale and Roddie more relaxed than he had been when he had gone in. It seemed to me that the very house itself heaved a sigh of relief.

Things were not over yet, however. The four of us were called immediately to the

Laird's study. Roddie, Charlotte, Richard and I, we all stood before him in a row for all the world like naughty children as he regarded us sternly from behind his desk.

"I hope," he began, "that we can now forget this most regrettable incident."

He rose from behind his desk and motioned us to seats. He himself stood before the great marble fireplace.

"I shall tell you what has been decided, or rather agreed," he said, inclining his head towards Roddie. "Roddie will make full use of the library here for his studies when he is home from Edinburgh. There seems little point in a room full of books that are not used. For this purpose, he will have access to the library at all times. In short, he will treat it as his own."

He paused and I glanced at Roddie, sure he would be delighted. For him to have all of the library to himself would be a wonderful thing. But his face bore that set look that I had seen before and I felt irritated that he could let his pride stand in the way of his progress. Richard's expression was equally shuttered.

"You, Kirsty," the Laird said, "will continue to share Charlotte's lessons, though I have to admit that you are outgrowing the schoolroom. Be that as it may, mornings will be spent reading or in some useful activity."

I looked at Charlotte to see how she would take this. Her mouth turned down at the words "useful activity". I wondered what the Laird had in mind.

"As for the afternoons," he went on, "I suggest they should be devoted to visiting not only the neighbouring estates but also the cottages in the village, as well as further afield on the Morach estate. There is much that two young women can accomplish by way of finding out what the needs of the tenants are and seeing what improvements can be made in their domestic situations. You will talk to the women of Morach and make their needs known to me. It is a long time since Morach had a resident laird and, though I know in your fathers time the tenants' needs were well looked after, I have the impression that things have been a bit slack since then."

I bent my head, unsure whether it was polite to agree with him. But I had to agree. There had been many instances when crofts had fallen into serious disrepair for the want of money and there were to my certain knowledge several families who could benefit from an improvement in their living conditions.

"In addition," he continued, "I have an idea it would be a good thing if you and Charlotte were to take an interest in the children on the estate. You, Kirsty, are of course well qualified for this and perhaps Charlotte can contribute the drawing and music skills she has acquired after so many years in the schoolroom."

Here he turned to Charlotte, who had the grace to blush, and I found myself wondering what on earth the children of Morach would make of the young Miss Munro in her silks and satins and strange accent. I could not easily see her in the role of Lady Bountiful.

The Laird did not say much more but, as we were leaving, he stopped us. "I will only add," he said, "that you are four young people together and that I have every hope that your association with one another will be beneficial to all."

I hoped so too, but I was not optimistic about it. I wished there was more friendship between Roddie and Richard. A tiny incident as we left the room made me even less hopeful.

Roddie and Richard approached the door at the same time. I saw Richard look at Roddie and raise his eyebrows slightly. Immediately Roddie stepped back to allow Richard to precede him. I sighed. For all Richard's good humour, I wondered if he too regarded Roddie as a peasant, a servant. If he did, it was usually well concealed and Roddie had certainly never mentioned it.

I turned to close the door behind us and caught the Laird's last words, spoken to himself.

"Please God it might be so!" he said.

I realized he was still talking about our "association" with one another. He had turned away and did not know I was still there so I merely drew the door to, not wishing to make a noise closing it. For some reason I was convinced he would not have wanted me to hear those words.

It was thus that the four of us were finally thrown together. And, looking back, it is as if Roddie was the missing piece in the jigsaw, the final part that made the pattern complete.

Chapter 7

In many ways the next two years were the happiest I had ever spent. I watched Mother relax in a way I had never known before and, in an odd way, my old ambition was fulfilled after all. It soon became obvious that Mademoiselle Lallande had taught Charlotte all she could, and I think it was with relief on all sides that she approached the Laird one day and told him of the position she had been offered in a very small and select school for young ladies in her own country. Still, I watched her go with genuine regret, for she had been kind to me. Not only that, but I must admit that she had also been a restraining influence on Charlotte and I was not at all sure of my ability to handle that young woman on my own.

As things turned out, I could not have been more fortunate. With Richard away at Oxford most of the year and Roddie in Edinburgh, Charlotte found my company poor recompense. Eventually the Laird agreed to invite guests from the neighbouring estates, and within a short time the castle was filled with house parties whose visits, of course, had to be returned. I would watch Charlotte with amazement on these occasions. She could be so charming when she wished.

I had some difficulty in persuading the Laird of my genuine reluctance to take part in the activities of the young people who flooded the house from time to time, or to accompany Charlotte on return visits. But eventually he saw that I had no wish to do so, especially when I explained the reason. The Dominie was growing older and I knew that he would welcome my help with the younger children. So I was able to please Mother by being at the castle, and myself by teaching at the village school whenever Charlotte's visiting allowed.

Roddie was not a good correspondent, but he came home when he could during his holidays. I watched in amazement as I noted his progress through the year. Each time I saw him he seemed to have grown taller and broader and his self-assurance grew to match. It was odd to see him and Richard together on their return to the castle, Richard full of the pranks and mischief he and his friends would get up to, and Roddie with a peace and maturity about him that I was glad to see. They seemed to approach their studies so differendy and yet I suppose that was only to be expected. For Roddie it was the gateway to a career, for Richard just something he was expected to do.

Charlotte hardly saw them during this time, she was away from home so much. That first summer was not an easy one. Charlotte was travelling with a neighbouring family in Europe, and the tension between Roddie and Richard was almost tangible. The Laird had insisted that Richard stay at home, though he too wanted to be off travelling. Roddie carried out his duties of teaching him the ways of the estate with a grim determination and Richard went back to Oxford in the autumn in no pleasant state of mind.

It was in late spring of the following year that the Laird got a letter from the Master of Richard's college. Charlotte was at home and we were having breakfast when the Laird's muttered exclamation caught our attention. He got up from the table and, with barely an apology, strode from the room.

I looked at Charlotte. "What can have happened?" I said.

She shook her head, looking concerned, for she was genuinely fond of her uncle.

"I'll go to him," she said.

It was some time before she returned.

"Richard is coming home," she said.

"I hope he is not unwell," I said.

To my surprise she laughed. "Unwell? No, he isn't unwell," she replied. "There has been a shooting accident. One of his friends was badly injured. A student prank that went wrong. Richard has been sent down."

I was reminded of Richard asking me if I would stand by him if he were in trouble, if he wandered off the straight and narrow. He was in trouble now.

"He will be very upset," I said.

Charlotte's mouth set in a tight line. "No doubt," she replied. "But if I were you I would not mention it to him."

When Richard came home there was a reserve about him that made me do as Charlotte said. I did not mention the accident. He said to me once, "Academic life doesn't suit me. I'm not like Roddie." And that was all he ever said on the subject. I did not pursue it. It was best forgotten.

With Richard at home, life at the castle was pleasanter. He exerted himself even more to be kind to me and I appreciated that. Mother had contracted an annoying little cough that would not go away and I was worried about her.

Roddie had not come home that year. In winter the roads had been impassable and he wrote in the spring to say that he had been asked to do some extra work, so it was summer before we saw him again, a full year since I had last seen him. And he was no longer a boy.

For Charlotte the change in him seemed even greater, for she had been away the previous summer. I smiled to myself as I saw her initial attitude of disdain crumble before Roddie's new-found self-assurance. She even refused to go off on a trip to the Swiss lakes with friends, a trip she had talked of constandy all the previous winter.

"Travelling on the continent in summer is so wearing," she said. "And I have never yet spent a full summer in Morach."

Richard laughed. "I wonder what makes this summer so different," he said. "Or should I say 'who'?"

Charlotte flushed and tossed her curls. She was prettier than ever.

"I really don't know what you're talking about, Richard," she said. "Is it so unusual to want to stay at home?"

He laughed again. "Only for you," he said.

"If Charlotte wants to stay at home, don't tease her, Richard," I said. "After all, it's the first time the four of us have been together for a long time."

I looked across at Roddie, lounging in a chair.

"That's right, Richard," he said. "And besides, Morach has at least as much to offer in summer entertainment as Europe has. Good heavens, there's the blanket wash!

Charlotte can see peasant rituals here to equal any she could see in Switzerland."

Charlotte turned on him, her eyes flashing with their old fire. "Roddie MacLelland, I haven't called you a peasant in years," she said indignantly.

Roddie laughed. "That's better, Charlotte," he said. "Ever since I came home I've been terrified in case you'd start calling me Mr MacLelland and invite me to carry your parasol."

Charlotte stamped her foot and flounced out of the room.

"Perhaps I shall go to Switzerland after all," she said as she went. "I can see that the civilizing process isn't quite complete yet."

But she didn't go to Switzerland, though she did go to the blanket wash.

The annual blanket wash was an institution in Morach as it was in every village and hamlet in the Highlands of Scotland. Every year, in summer, a huge peat fire was built between flat stones close to the point where the stream flowed into the loch. Then an enormous pot of water was set to boil on it. Big wooden tubs were rilled with water from the stream and the pot was heated to a temperature that allowed the girls to get into it and trample the blankets in the soapy water.

Older women were there to help and the children had a wonderful time, playing around the stream and being scolded for getting too near the fire. The young men of the village would come and lounge around, joking with the bare-legged girls as they trampled the blankets, singing in time to their steps. It was one of the events of the year and the whole village gathered beyond the lych-gate where the stream flowed fastest and the loch made the rinsing of the blankets easy.

Charlotte was horrified by the whole thing, from the fact that I was going to help Mother to the sight of the girls, their skirts kilted and their legs bare to the view of the young men as they continued blithely with their work.

"You don't mean to tell me you're going to go down there and tramp blankets in a bucket, do you?" she said disbelievingly. "Why, it's ridiculous!"

"Charlotte," I said, "my mother is not well at the moment. Her cough is getting worse and the work would be too heavy for her alone. Of course I shall go and help her."

"But why on earth not bring your wretched blankets here and wash them in the laundry?" she said. "I take it we do have a laundry?"

I smiled. "Yes, you do," I said. "But the blanket wash is a tradition in the village."

I could not think how to explain to her what the blanket wash meant to the women of the village, even to Mother who regarded herself as different. It was a great occasion.

Summer was well and truly with us and winter not to be thought of until the peat cutting came. For a few short weeks, hills and loch basked in the warmth of the sun and the long, light evenings of the summer dusk lasted almost until midnight. It was a time of relaxation for Morach and the blanket wash provided a days companionship and fun for the whole village. When the evening came and everyone began to walk home, tired but pleasandy so, there was a sense of community about the village that would bind it together for another year. And next day, as blankets were hung out to dry and bleach in the sun, there was a sense of work well done.

There was no point in trying to explain this to Charlotte who did not know or even care how her clothes were laundered. So I merely insisted that I would go to the blanket wash and left it at that.

Mother and I carried our large wooden tub down together. She looked happy as we joined the other women walking down towards the loch, happier than she had looked since Father died, and I was glad that I had agreed to go to the castle. I was also worried about her for she had grown thinner and seemed to tire easily, but when I mentioned this to her she would have none of it.

"Nonsense, Kirsty!" she said. "Why, look at the colour I have in my cheeks. I haven't looked so pretty since I was a girl. It's the soft life at the castle that's making me lazy."

It was true she did have a pretty colour and her eyes had a brightness in them that was new to me. But still I was concerned, for nothing could have made her lazy and I had seen her come home from the castle more tired than she had ever been by less work. I held my tongue, however, but thought I might speak to Roddie's grandmother about it. Perhaps she would give Mother one of her famous herbal tonics.

I found the opportunity when the work stopped for a picnic lunch and the women left their labours, moving away from the peat fire to the cool of the loch shore. I perched on a convenient boulder next to old Mrs MacLelland.

"Ah, good day, Kirsty my dear! And how is life at the castle?" she enquired.

I made a face. "I imagine you'll hear enough of that from Roddie," I said. "He spends a good part of his time in the library there now."

"Ach, that boy!" she said proudly. "It's books, books, books for him. I never knew the like of it."

"He's doing a wonderful thing," I said. "Why, there isn't another man in the village could do what he's doing. Edinburgh is going to turn him into a gentleman."

Her eyes came round sharply to my face. "Is that why he's doing it?" she said. "Is that what he says?"

I was taken aback by the vehemence in her voice. "No," I said consideringly. "No, I don't think so."

Her eyes held mine. It was clear that her question was serious and I did my best to give her a serious answer.

"I don't know why he's doing it, Mrs MacLelland," I said at last, "but I know that there *is* a reason. I don't think it's just so that he can be a lawyer. Oh, I know he does want to be one, but there's something else driving him, something deep inside him, and I don't know what it is."

Her eyes moved away from mine and I felt as if I had been released. A chill swept over me and I shivered slighdy. What I had said had been true, I knew that, but it had surprised me to know it. I had not thought of Roddie's reasons before, except to think of him as a clever boy who wanted to get on. I knew now that there was more to it than that, but I did not know what that was.

It seemed she had finished with the subject, however, for she said, "And how is your mother, Kirsty?" and I was able to tell her how I felt about Mother's health.

She promised to make up a tonic and give it to Roddie for her and at once I felt easier in my mind. I rose to go and, as I did so, my eye was caught by the sight of the Druid Island where the oaks stood tall and green in the sunlight.

"Isn't it a lovely sight?" I said.

She looked out towards it. "Evil often looks beautiful from the outside, Kirsty. Places as well as people."

I was shocked. "Evil?" I said. "Surely you don't believe all those stories about the island?"

Her eyes came round again. She had extraordinary eyes, very clear but so dark as to be almost black.

"It isn't the stories that make the place evil, Kirsty, but the foolishness of those that *do* believe in them," she said.

"Roddie doesn't like the island," I said.

"No," she agreed.

"He told me why once," I went on.

Her *eyes* came round to rest on me. "He told you about his father?" she said.

I was confused. "Not exactly," I said. "I didn't think he knew who his father was." I stopped, appalled at what I had said.

Her *eyes* met mine, unflinching. "He knows," she said.

She turned back, her eyes once more on the island, and I would have spoken. But I saw that even if I had, she would not have heard, she was so intent on her thoughts.

A voice hailed me and I turned to see Richard with Effie giggling by his side, her feet bare and pink from tramping the tub. Even Effie had come to the blanket wash for the fun of it. I made my way towards them along the shore.

"Why, Richard!" I said. "What brings you here?"

He laughed down at Effie and said teasingly, "I was lured here by the thought of a sight of Effie's bare ankles."

I made a disapproving face and Effie giggled delightedly again.

"Losh, Mr Richard," she said, "you mustn't say such things! You'll make Kirsty jealous."

He bent and said something in her ear and she blushed scarlet and hid her face in her apron. As she did so a small green-covered book fell out. I was surprised. Effie had never been a great reader. Then I realized what it was. It was the book Richard had shown me, the one about the legends of Morach and the Druid Island. I wondered again if it was the same book Roddie had spoken of years ago. She picked it up and slipped it quickly back in her apron as another voice broke in.

"Effie, your mother is looking for you," said Roddie.

I looked up. He and Charlotte stood on the grassy slope above the shingle. Roddie was watching me intendy and I wondered if he had heard Effie's last remark.

Effie gathered up her skirts and made her way up the slope with a sulky look.

"You needn't be so Lord of the Manor with me, Roddie MacLelland," she said as she passed him. "Even if you do have the run of the castle." And she looked meaningfully at Charlotte.

I saw his face harden, but he leapt lighdy on to the shingle and held out his hands to help Charlotte down. She was in pale lilac with a most becoming picture hat and her shoes were totally unsuitable for walking on grass, much less shingle. She put her hands out and allowed herself to be almost lifted down from the bank. I saw Roddie's arm tighten around her waist for a moment as she stumbled and a faint blush mounted her cheeks as she looked up to thank him. I found myself wondering if Effie's jibe at Roddie had found its mark but Charlotte had recovered herself.

"Really, Richard!" she said. "You allow yourself to be overfamiliar with that girl."

Richard looked pointedly at Roddie's arm which was just disengaging itself from her waist.

"I agree that it is not seemly to dally with servants," he drawled and the point was not lost on her. "But silly little Effie was more accurate than she realized. I *did* think it might make Kirsty jealous. She continues to resist all my charms."

There was a muffled sound from above us and I turned to see Effie looking down at me. She spun on her heel and strode away, but not before I had seen the look in her eyes.

"Richard!" I said. "What a thing to say! She heard you. You've hurt her feelings."

"Effie's feelings?" he said, as if the idea puzzled him. "But it's true." He gave me a mournful look. "I've tried and tried. I believe you have given your heart to another."

I was suddenly impatient. Richard could be quite callous sometimes.

"My heart is my own and quite intact," I said.

Roddie's voice broke in again.

"Which is more than can be said for Effie's," he said. "Charlotte is right, Richard. She is only a simple village girl. You will give her ideas above her station."

"You would know about that, I suppose," Richard said, an edge of anger in his voice. I gasped, but he said almost as quickly, "I'm sorry, Roddie. I shouldn't have said that. But your job is to teach me about the estate, not to run my personal life." He looked rueful as he held out his hand to Roddie. "That particular occupation is rather oversubscribed."

Roddie hesitated only a moment. His eyes locked with Richard's for an instant and I saw the old rivalry flare between them again. Then Roddie accepted the handshake and the apology.

"We'd best be getting up the hill," he said. "There's been a wildcat worrying the sheep and I've an idea I know where its lair is." He turned to me then. "You'll see Charlotte back to the castle, Kirsty? It's not right she should be wandering about on her own."

I nodded as Charlotte protested.

"I'm not a child, Roddie," she said. "I'm nineteen, for goodness' sake!"

He looked at her gravely. "I'm well aware of your age, Charlotte," he said. "It's your position I have in mind."

He and Richard turned away with a wave and I looked at Charlotte. She was looking after them, her eyes bright and her mouth set in a stubborn line.

"Charlotte. . ." I began, but I got no further.

She turned on me and stamped her foot. "Don't say it. Just don't say anything, Kirsty. Oh, why do you people have to be so proud and stubborn?"

I almost laughed. Coming from her, that was pretty rich. But I didn't laugh for I was too surprised. It was very foolish of me, but I simply hadn't realized she was in love with Roddie. Or perhaps it was not so surprising. Charlotte was the niece of the Laird of Morach and the Loch, and she had never been slow to make her attitude towards the Laird's tenants plain. Oh, I had known she was attracted to Roddie, but I had considered it a passing fancy, a mild flirtation. But what I saw in her eyes was no romantic whim. She really cared for him.

It was as the last of us were making our way homeward in the long twilight that the news came. Charlotte and I were approaching the castle gates, having seen Mother back to the cottage with her blankets, when Effie came running down the drive to meet us. Her fact was white with fear, no excitement there now, as she almost threw herself on us.

"Have you heard?" she said. "Oh, you'll not have heard! Oh, it's terrible!"

"Oh, for goodness' sake, Effie," Charlotte said. "What on earth are you talking about?"

Effie cast a venomous look at Charlotte, but even that could not disguise her distress. I grasped her by the shoulders and almost shook the words out of her.

"Heard what, Effie?" I said. "What has happened?"

"There's been an accident," she replied. "On the hill. They're bringing him down now and we don't know whether he's dead or alive."

I felt my mouth go dry and my heart began to hammer in my breast.

"Who?" I said and the voice did not sound like my own. "Who has been hurt?"

Chapter 8

For a long moment time seemed to stand still. Then Effie spoke.

"Roddie," she said. "Richard was trying to shoot the wildcat in the half-light. It was attacking Roddie."

I let go of her shoulders, my mind in a whirl as she broke down in noisy sobs, and I turned to Charlotte. She was white, her eyes darkened by her emotion. I put my hands out to steady her and felt her own cold hand clutch mine. She was not looking at me but beyond me at something I could not see.

"Oh, no!" she said. "Not again." And she fainted.

Effie began to wail once more and I turned to her.

"Stop that, Effie!" I said sharply. "It'll do no good." I bent to rummage in Charlotte's reticule. I found, as I knew I would, a small bottle of smelling-salts, and quickly uncapped it. As I did so, I heard the sounds of carriage wheels and, thrusting the bottle at Effie, motioned her to continue. I waited as MacCrimmon brought the carriage to a halt.

"Losh, Kirsty, what's happened now?" he said, his eyes round with wonder as he looked at Charlotte, lying in her crumpled silks with Effie bending over her.

"It's nothing," I said. "She merely fainted when she heard the news."

"Fainted?" he said and there was a spark of interest behind his eyes.

I bit my lip. "It wasn't clear at first who had been hurt," I said. That was true enough.

"Och, she thought it was the young laird?" he said. "Poor lassie. That must have given her a shock."

"Have you any news?" I asked, looking up at him.

He shook his head. "No more than you have, it seems," he said. "They've gone up the hill to fetch him down. The young Munro arrived down in a terrible state but he's gone off to lead them to the spot. I'm just away to fetch the doctor."

But for his last words, I would have detained him, have asked for more information, but what good would knowing more do? It was better that he was on his way as quickly as possible. He gathered up the reins as I stepped back.

"Does his grandmother know?" I called after him.

The words came floating back through the gathering darkness. "One of the lassies has gone for her," he said.

I looked after him as he turned through the great gates. It would soon be dark and the moor was a treacherous place. Please God they found him before the last of the light had gone! My eyes rose to the line of hills, their oudine blurred now and merging with the skyline. I thought of Roddie lying up there, injured, and the futile lanterns of the searchers. How well had he taught Richard? Would he be able to find the place again? My attention was distracted by a low moan, then Charlotte's voice.

"For goodness' sake, Effie, take that evil-smelling thing away!" she snapped. At least she seemed quite recovered.

Between us, Effie and I supported her up to the castle. Effie was alive with questions she did not dare ask. I made sure I rebuked her for not making clear who had been hurt.

"Charlotte thought Richard had been injured," I said.

Effie looked sideways at me. "If you say so," she said.

"I *do* say so," I replied.

I didn't want Effie spreading rumours. When we reached the castle I was glad I had warned her, for Charlotte's face was paper white and her eyes huge with apprehension. I took her at once to the small drawing-room.

"I'll get some tea," Effie said, looking at Charlotte. "She looks as if she could do with it."

I nodded. The Laird, it seemed, had gone with the searchers. When Effie came back I watched carefully as the warmth of the fire and the tea brought some colour back into Charlotte's face.

There was something troubling me, something I had to ask her.

"Charlotte," I said. "What did you mean 'not again'?"

Her head drooped, the fire gleaming brighdy on the fair hair. Golden, Roddie had called it.

"I don't know what you mean," she said.

"Perhaps you do not remember," I said. "But you did say those words. I wondered whether you were thinking of the incident at Oxford when Richard was sent down."

She gazed at me for a moment, her eyes wide. "Yes," she said. "Richard is so unlucky."

Effie snorted. "Roddie was the one that got hurt," she said. "It seems to me he's the unlucky one."

Charlotte looked as if she might faint again and I felt myself losing patience with both of them.

"These were accidents," I said. "Nothing to do with luck." I turned to Charlotte. "Surely you can't believe superstitious nonsense like that?"

"Things happen," Charlotte said. "There are things you cannot understand, Kirsty."

"I can understand how you could frighten yourself into fits believing someone is unlucky," I said tartly.

Effie broke in. "You might not believe in superstition, Kirsty," she said, "but Richard does."

I remembered the little green book and I turned to Effie to ask her about it. But I did not get the chance.

It was then that we heard sounds in the hall and we sat frozen for a moment before flying to the door. The scene etched itself in my memory. The great hall, so large in reality, seemed to shrink as I looked at the group that stood there. The lamps flared in the draught from the doorway and threw grotesque shadows on the walls. The Laird was there, looking strained and tired. Ewan, Effie's brother, and several of the estate workers were lowering to the floor a makeshift stretcher.

I could hardly bear to look and when I did an involuntary gasp escaped my lips. Roddie lay there, his face bereft of all colour except where the blood lay in a dark clotted streak from his head and down his cheek. His eyes were closed and, as the stretcher was settled on the floor, the blanket that covered him slipped. It was a moment before I realized that the strange dark stain that covered his breast must also be blood.

I felt the beginnings of panic rise in me. Then, it seemed to me miraculously, his head turned and his eyes opened and looked straight into mine and in my mind the words began to beat – *He is not dead! He is not dead!*

The scene, frozen for those few moments, shattered and broke as a small figure said from the doorway, "And do you want him to die of the cold on that stone floor? Away with you and get him to a warm bed! I've brought my medicines."

At once, all was normality again and the sense of relief was almost tangible as we turned as one to see old Mrs MacLelland standing there, her black eyes flashing and a bundle under her arm. I almost giggled at the incongruous sight she made, a small, indomitable black figure in the great hall. I suppose it was relief.

Immediately all was bustle and motion and Roddie was carried upstairs, his grandmother following on behind, giving instructions as she went.

"I'll need hot water and clean linen and as many hot bricks as you can manage, wrapped in flannel, mind. . ."

I turned to Charlotte but her eyes were elsewhere. I looked where she was looking and, for the first time, noticed Richard. His clothes were stained and dirty and his hair stood comically on end. But that was not what caught my attention. It was the look that passed between him and Charlotte. It lasted only a moment. Then, without a word, he turned and followed the little party upstairs and Charlotte turned back to the small drawing-room. I could not ask her what that look meant. I did not know where to begin. But it troubled me. It had been so full of a meaning I did not understand.

We found the Laird in the drawing-room, a glass of whisky in his hand. He looked haggard. Charlotte moved immediately to his side and he put out a hand to touch her bright hair.

"It's all right," he said. "It's going to be all right."

She relaxed against him and I wondered to myself, does he know of her feelings for Roddie? Surely not, when even I who have been so much in their company have only just realized it.

They stood together for a moment before she said, "Have you discovered what happened?"

He moved towards a side table and poured himself another glass of whisky.

"It seems they found the wildcat and cornered it," he said at last. "It made a spring for Roddie and in the half-light Richard fired on it."

She turned towards him eagerly, but he stayed her with a gesture.

"We shall have to get the whole story tomorrow. Roddie has not been able to speak much. He is in considerable pain."

"Tomorrow?" I said. "Then he is not badly hurt?"

The Laird turned towards me, his face all concern. "No, Kirsty," he said. "I don't think it's anything to worry about. I'm sorry. I should have said sooner. You are such friends."

"But his head. . ." I said. "And the blood on his chest."

He made a dismissive gesture. "He hit a stone as he fell," he said. "Richard panicked. Thought he was dead. When we arrived he was conscious again. The wounds on his chest are from shot. Painful to pick out, but not unduly serious."

I heaved a sigh of relief. It had looked so bad as he lay on the floor of the great hall. Charlotte moved towards her uncle.

"You should go and change," she said. "You'll catch cold if you don't get out of those wet things."

The Laird looked at his legs and feet and smiled at the sight. They were wet and muddy to the knees. Even in summer the hills were never entirely dry.

"I'll wait for the doctor," he said. "MacCrimmon has gone to fetch him."

The doctor arrived soon afterwards. He went upstairs immediately with the Laird while Charlotte and I huddled by the fire and waited for news. I did not speak of the depth of her concern for Roddie. I did not want to. I was too busy with my own feelings. When Effie had said those words – *There's been an accident on the hill* – what had I thought? Which of them came first to my mind?

Only half an hour had passed by the time they returned, the Laird leading the way, the doctor and Mrs MacLelland behind, discussing the patient. It was evident that the doctor held Roddies grandmother in high regard and that she took this as only natural. Dr Baird assured us that there was nothing to worry about and refused refreshment, saying there was a confinement in Fort William he had to get back to.

"Not difficult in the usual sense, Laird," he said, his ruddy face breaking into a smile. "Nothing a woman couldn't see to. But she's wealthy and delicately nurtured so I'll have to go myself."

His eyes twinkled mischievously in Charlotte's direction and I saw her blush at such an indelicate subject, then he took his leave. The Laird led Mrs MacLelland to a chair by the fire and settled her there.

"You'll have a dram?" he said, and it wasn't so much a question as a request.

She nodded her head regally, silting there in her black with her eyes that saw everything.

"I will," she said.

He turned to us and we took the dismissal.

"Ewan will see you safely home, Kirsty," he said. "Your mother will be worried, not knowing where you are."

Mrs MacLelland spoke.

"I sent word to your mother, Kirsty, but she'll be waiting up for you all the same. Don't go worrying her now, for Roddies going to be just fine. There's no need to be upsetting yourself."

I nodded. Somehow it seemed perfectly natural that she should know and accept exactly how this would affect Mother. I was to accept it also. I would not worry Mother by being over-anxious about Roddie. As I left she stopped me once more.

"Kirsty," she said, "I've given your mother some medicine. See that she takes it every day, there's a good girl."

I looked into her eyes and saw such kindness that I could do no more than nod once again. It was all that needed to be said. I would not worry her and I would see that she took her medicine. Ewan was waiting for me so I did not have a chance to do more than say a quick goodbye to Charlotte.

"I'll be up first thing in the morning," I said.

"He'll want to see you, I expect," she replied.

And with those words we became rivals.

Chapter 9

It was decided that Roddie would stay at Blair Morach until he was fully recovered. At first he would not hear of it, but Charlotte put the point most forcibly next day.

"You cannot allow your grandmother to run around after you, Roddie," she said. "She is an old woman and you are not in any fit state to do anything for yourself."

He regarded her levelly from the chair in which he was sitting. His head was swathed in bandages and his left arm strapped across his chest to prevent undue strain on his injured shoulder.

"Ah, Charlotte!" he said. "It is commendable that you should be so concerned for my grandmother's welfare, but surely a witch would be able to overcome such a trivial handicap as age."

She blushed scarlet. "I apologized for that a long time ago, Roddie, and I think it most unfair that you should bring it up again."

He extended his right hand to her and she put her own in his.

"That's better, Charlotte," he said. "I like you fighting. It suits you so much better than pious thoughtfulness."

She withdrew her hand quickly and was within an inch of stamping her foot as she said, "Oh, go to the devil! Why should I care whether you get well or not?"

He let forth a great bellow of laughter and then winced as the movement hurt his shoulder.

"And why should you?" he said.

She did stamp her foot this time. "I don't," she said. "And anyway, I should have thought the library would be enough attraction for you here."

I watched from the window seat as she swept from the room in her customary fashion. She halted at the door for a moment as his voice reached her.

"And not the only attraction," he said softly.

I saw a smile form on her lips and she turned once more towards him, then her expression grew sulky and she was gone.

I turned to Roddie. He was looking at me somewhat ruefully.

"Really, Roddie!" I said. "You should not tease her so."

He waved his good arm in a dismissive gesture.

"She's a spoilt miss," he said. "And she's used to being the centre of attraction. She's bored, that's all."

"I'm not so sure," I replied carefully. "Has it not occurred to you that she might be genuinely fond of you?

He laughed again. "Ah, Kirsty!" he said. "And aren't I the only young man she has to practise her charms on apart from her cousin? And there seems little love lost between them. Put that young woman and me in a drawing-room in London or Edinburgh, full of eligible young men, and she'd take no more notice of me than if I were the butler."

I didn't pursue the subject. If he wanted to think that, then let him. After all, who was to say he was wrong? Nor did I want to know whether it mattered to him – not yet. I was more interested in what he had said about Charlotte and Richard.

"Charlotte and Richard don't get on well, you know," I said. "And yet there seems no reason for it."

His face darkened. "There's something between them," he said. "I've felt it now and again and if I didn't think my knock on the head had made me fanciful, I'd say it was fear."

I was about to protest when the door opened and Richard walked in. I felt immediately guilty because we had been talking about him and I could feel the colour rising in my face.

"Kirsty!" he said. "Is that blush for me? Careful or you'll be giving me hope."

I murmured a rebuke, but was saved by Roddie.

"I have to thank you, Richard, for saving my life," he said.

Richard looked at him sharply, then smiled.

"Please don't," he said. "I nearly killed you as it was. It's this odd half-light you have up here. Damned awkward to shoot by."

I laughed. "It's called the gloaming, Richard," I said. "The day lasts longer in summer the farther north you are. But Roddies right. A wildcat goes straight for the throat. He wouldn't have stood a chance."

"Oh, nonsense!" Richard said. "I'm only sorry I got you instead of the animal. The shot did no more than frighten it away. It's still out there somewhere."

"We'll go after it again," said Roddie quietly.

Richard's eyes came up to meet his. "But not at dusk," he said jokingly.

"No," said Roddie. "Not at dusk."

The fire shifted and settled and I looked towards it.

"It'll be the peat-cutting soon, Roddie," I said. "Will you be well enough to do your grandmother's?"

"And yours too," he said.

I protested. "Don't be ridiculous," I said. "I'm quite able to do that myself."

"Your mother won't be able to help you," he said.

I nodded, still looking into the glowing heart of the fire. "Your grandmother's medicine seems to be doing her good," I said.

I looked at him for confirmation, but saw only compassion in his eyes. Then Richard said, "We'll get Doctor Baird over to see her if you like, Kirsty, though I must admit I thought she was looking in the pink. All that healthy colour she has."

I couldn't speak, but Roddie spoke for me, saying for the first time that dreadful word that I had so far managed to put from my mind.

"Consumption," he said. That was all. Just one word. It hung in the air, out at last, the thing I had been dreading.

"Oh, I say!" said Richard. "I'm most awfully sorry, Kirsty. Does she know?"

I was close to tears. "She must," I said. "The signs are unmistakable, but she has never admitted it. Perhaps she thinks I don't know what that bright colour in her cheeks means. It seems so unjust that it makes her look so well and all the time..." My voice trailed off and I rose. "I think I'll take a walk," I said.

Richard made a movement towards me. "I'll come with you," he said.

"No," I said. "I'd rather be alone."

At the door, Roddie's voice stayed me. "It had to be said, Kirsty," he said and I looked at him, at the pity in his eyes, and nodded.

"I know that," I replied. "Thank you, Roddie. It's better that I should face up to it now, that I should be prepared."

I wanted to say that it was better that it came from him than from anyone else, but I didn't. Instead, I put on heavy outdoor boots and wrapped a shawl round me and went up on to the hill.

I sat there for a long time, watching the birds wheeling and dipping, listening to the hundreds of tiny streams that made their tortuous way down to the river. I looked down on the only place I had known. It was not the only place Mother had known and she had not always been happy here, but it was the place where she would die and I wept for the sadness of it. She had worked so hard since Father had died, going without so that I should be clothed and have enough to eat without taking charity. She had worked so hard to keep us "respectable".

I lifted my head. Morach and the glen were a blur before me, and I heard my voice raised above the murmur of the streams and the screaming of the swifts.

"Was it worth it?" I cried into the empty air and all my anger was in that cry.

Then a figure wavered before my blurred vision and dropped beside me and a strong arm was around my shoulders. I put my head on his good shoulder and cried out all my anger and all my sorrow. It was a long time before I could speak.

"You shouldn't be here," I said ungratefully. "You should be resting. You're not fit to be out yet."

I looked up into Roddie's face. It had been a hard climb for him in his state and the strain showed in the pallor of his skin and the fine lines round his mouth. He bent his head close to mine.

"And would you have me tucked up like an invalid in front of the fire when you are in so much pain up here?" he said.

It was then that he kissed me. Not with the urgency and passion that Richard had shown, but gently and with infinite tenderness. I wanted to cling to him and ask him to be there always and take care of me, but of course I didn't.

Instead, I said, "Thank you, Roddie. You're a good friend."

He smoothed my hair back from my face. "If you should ever need me, Kirsty, I'll be there," he said. He made to get to his feet and the movement must have hurt him, for there was a bitter twist to his mouth. "After all, that's what friends are for."

Charlotte was at the door waiting for us when we got back and her look was frosty as she said to me, "Kirsty, how could you be so thoughtless with Roddie in the state he's in?"

It was no use protesting. She was in full flight as she sheperded him into the house and fussed around him, tucking him into his chair by the fire and bringing him books.

Roddie was enjoying himself hugely and even I found myself smiling as he said with a wink at me, "You're right, Charlotte. I do feel a little weak."

At once she was all concern, bending over him. His eyes were closed and he did indeed look pale. Then one eye opened, the eyebrow above it arched humorously, and he said, "Just smooth my brow a little, Charlotte, there's a good girl," and she stormed from the room.

He looked after her, his face comically quizzical as he said, "Does that girl ever leave a room normally?"

"Not when you're around," I said. "And don't come complaining to me if you come off worse in this little game, Roddie MacLelland. You're playing with fire."

He smiled up at me. "Ach, it *is* just a game", he said, "to while away a poor invalid's lonely hours."

I made a face at him as I too left.

"Watch you don't get burned," I said.

"No fear of that," he said. "I'm well protected."

But I wondered if he was. After all, by his own admission he found her pretty and Charlotte was not one to be thwarted once she had set a course. Perhaps he was right. He was, after all, attractive and there was nothing in the way of competition here at Morach. Maybe she was just amusing herself or believing herself in love out of boredom. But somehow I doubted it. And, besides, it was not something I wanted to think about, I told myself again. I seemed to have been telling myself that rather a lot recently.

Thanks to Charlotte, Roddie made an excellent recovery. She dragooned him into eating vast quantities of invalid food and struck up an alliance with old Mrs MacLelland. They made an odd pair, bent together over discussions on his progress. Charlotte was a picture of vibrant youth, her bright hair and light, pretty clothes contrasting oddly with the old woman's sombre black. Still, between them they had him on his feet and fit much sooner than Doctor Baird had predicted. But there were always battles.

The fiercest was over the peat cutting. Roddie would have none of this sitting around reading books and eating what he referred to as "pap" while the peats were needing to be cut. The battle raged all over the house as Charlotte tried to dissuade him.

"Losh, Kirsty!" Effie said to me. "Has Miss Charlotte no decency to shout after him like that?"

"She's only concerned for his health, Effie," I said. "She's quite right. He isn't fit to go digging peats with that shoulder."

She gave me a very old-fashioned look. "Roddie MacLelland will do exactly as he pleases," she said. "And if she doesn't know that by now, she never will. If you ask me, she's got more than his shoulder on her mind."

I turned to her sharply. "I didn't ask you, Effie, and you'd do better to keep your thoughts to yourself," I said.

I saw surprise leap in her eyes, then a sly look as she said, "There now, and wasn't I thinking there was a match brewing between you and the young laird."

"Oh, don't be so nonsensical!" I said, goaded by her.

She bridled. "Acting the lady already, Kirsty?" she said spitefully. "Well, don't be surprised if he finds the waiting a wee bit hard to take. He's not one to be kept on a string," and she flounced off.

I gritted my teeth, annoyed that I had given her more fuel for her gossiping tongue.

It was true that with Roddie's invalid status and Charlotte's nursing, Richard had more time on his hands and a great deal of it had been spent with me. But I had consciously been keeping him at arm's length.

There was something in Richard that frightened me a little – a violence of feeling in him. On the surface he was the pleasant-est of people, but underneath I could sense a darker side to him. It showed itself in small ways. He was swift to anger and equally quick to disguise it. To me he was always charming, but there was an intensity about him that I felt was barely held in check and I was frightened to release that intensity by seeming to return his regard.

Or maybe I was imagining the extent of his affection for me. If what Roddie said about Charlotte being bored and interested in him only because there was no rival was true, then surely the same could apply to Richard. Of one thing I was certain: I liked Richard, I had been attracted to him in the past. But it was Roddie's kiss that I found myself thinking of more and more, not Richard's.

I shook myself out of such thoughts. It was unseemly when Mother was getting weaker by the day. Even the light work she did now at the castle tired her beyond measure, but I had not the heart to tell her she must stop. She looked so well, thin but with that beautiful transparent bloom of health that is such a cruel prelude to an inevitable end. One thing I had insisted on: she was not to come peat cutting. Richard had promised to help me and I had accepted his offer gratefully. Mother, of course, thought it hardly right that he should take his place among the people of the village like that. But the Laird was entirely in agreement and, when he spoke to Mother about it, she could do no more than assent.

Roddie of course did go to the peat cutting. There was no reason why he should not, for he was quite fit and would be off back to Edinburgh soon. He had gone back to his grandmother's house after Charlotte's last tirade, saying that he would recover better if he didn't have to use up his energy shouting at her, and Charlotte, duly chastened, gave in.

We assembled on the moor where the purple was scarred with black in the places where the peats had been cut. It is hard work. A special spade is used to cut the soft peats which are laid out in rows to dry before being built up into small heaps. Eventually they are taken on creels on the backs of women and children to be stacked near the houses to provide fuel for the next year.

Richard made a brave attempt, but it was beyond him to stay all day. When I saw his hands I felt guilty, realizing how unfitted he was for the work. There were great blisters on his palms and his fingers were bleeding in places. I was examining them, exclaiming at the pain he must be in, when Roddie approached. He looked at Richard's hands and smiled, not unkindly.

"Each to his own, Richard," he said. "You'd best away home and get Charlotte to see to those hands. She'll be missing her nursing."

"I don't mind the pain," Richard said shortly.

"I didn't say you did," said Roddie. "But you'll be worse than useless with hands like that. And you'll just worry Kirsty."

"And you're so concerned for Kirsty, aren't you?" Richard said.

"Roddie's right, Richard," I said quickly as Richard's cheeks flushed with anger. "You can't work with your hands in that state. You've been wonderful coming to help at all."

Richard drew a hand over his forehead, leaving a peaty streak. The anger was gone as swiftly as it had come.

"I feel such a fool," he said, gesturing to the moor that lay around us. It was dotted with small black figures digging the winter's warmth from the earth. "Why, there are children still digging!"

"It's knowing how it's done," said Roddie. "That's all. You're not used to it. Kirsty and I were brought up to this."

"Kirsty and you," Richard repeated. For a moment his eyes were far away. Then he shook his head. "I'll be off then – if I'm not needed."

We looked after him as he strode across the moor.

"Poor Richard!" I said. "It was so good of him to come."

"Ach, don't you worry about him," said Roddie, grinning as he looked at the ill-assorted shapes of the peats Richard had dug. "His pride is giving him more pain than his blisters."

I snorted. "You're a fine one to talk about pride!" I said. "You're not short of it yourself."

"I've enough of it to know what I can handle," he said. "I don't play the gentleman. He shouldn't play the peasant."

I looked at him in surprise. "That still rankles, doesn't it?" I said.

He grasped my meaning at once. "It's how she regards the people of Morach," he replied.

"Not you," I said. "Not now."

He looked across the moor at the workers bent over the earth.

120

"I'm one of them, Kirsty," he said. "I always will be. As I said to Richard – each to his own."

Suddenly I didn't want to hear any more.

"Are your grandmother's peats dug?" I asked.

His gaze shifted from the moor. "There was no lack of helpers," he said with a smile. "Not for her."

I smiled back. "No, there wouldn't be," I said.

The thought lay unspoken between us. For the wife of Jamie Strachan who was "different" and had kept herself apart there were no helpers. Not that they weren't willing, but after so many rebuffs they would have to be asked and it wasn't my place to do the asking.

Between us, Roddie and I did well with the cutting but it was far into the evening before we were done. The light was almost gone from the sky as we stacked the last peat. There had been no suggestion from Roddie that I should go home and leave it to him and I admired him for that. It was my home the peats were for and right that I should do the work.

As the last peat was stacked, we straightened and I saw him put a hand to his shoulder, but I made no comment. The moor lay deserted before us, the heather a dark mass on the hill, and a breeze had sprung up, light but with an edge to it that spoke of autumn. The summers did not last long in Morach. In our nostrils was the smell of freshly-cut peat and, as sometimes happens, I felt a great surge of love for this place of mine. I raised my hands and loosed the scarf that had tied up my hair, letting it fall around my shoulders. I lifted my face to the breeze and closed my eyes the better to savour it, saying to Roddie, "Do you not love this place?"

He touched my face lightly with his fingertips.

"Kirsty Strachan," he said, "your face is filthy and your clothes no better, but your hair is the colour of the raven's wing and you are beautiful."

My eyes flew open in surprise, but he was looking at me so gravely that I said nothing.

"Do you care for him?" he said.

I looked deep into his eyes, shadowed now in the waning light.

"Richard?" I hesitated but I could not take my eyes from his and I found the answer so surely that I wondered I had ever been in any doubt. "No," I said. "Not in the way you mean."

It was as if the world had been stilled for us and now, as he let out a long, deep sigh, his arms came round me and I was crushed against him, and this time there was no tenderness in his kiss but a passion and a longing I had not known existed. I felt his hands move over me as I abandoned myself to his embrace and heard murmurings that I did not trouble to try to understand as his lips touched my cheeks, my eyes and again my mouth. At last he lifted his head.

"I thought it was Charlotte," I said on a long breath.

His mouth curved in a slow smile. "No," he said. "Charlotte is not for me."

"You flirt with her," I said.

"I have my reasons," he replied.

"What reasons?" I asked.

His mouth tightened a little. "I do not want to make Richard too jealous," he said and smiled.

I did not answer and he spoke again.

"Will you trust me?" he said.

"Yes," I said, though I was uneasy at his asking.

His eyes searched my face and what they saw must have satisfied him for he said, "You will wait for me, Kirsty."

And I said, "I will."

We came off the hill then, not speaking or touching, and he left me at my mother's door. I watched him disappear into the darkness and I wondered to myself, why is it that I am not ablaze with happiness? For I knew now that there was no other man for me. Why then did a small insistent voice ring in my ear – "each to his own".

Chapter 10

In many ways the rest of that summer seems like a dream to me now. It's as if I moved through it without being part of it in any real sense. Mother was growing increasingly fragile but still insisted on going up to the castle though Effie's mother assured me that she was given as little work as possible.

"It's as well to let her come up, lassie," Mrs Robertson said. "After all, what would she do at home? She'd just work there and at least here we can be sure she doesn't tire herself too much."

I was still unconvinced. "But she's getting so frail, Mrs Robertson," I said. "I can't help feeling guilty, letting her come up here instead of resting at home."

"Kirsty, you know she wouldn't rest at home," Mrs Robertson said. "Let her come up as long as possible. I'll see she isn't overstrained."

"That's kind of you," I said. "I know it isn't easy. She's very independent."

She looked at me sympathetically. "She hasn't taken help. Not since your father died," she said. "And who's to say she's wrong? She didn't have an easy time of it when she first came here."

At once my interest was caught. "She never speaks of that time, Mrs Robertson," I said. "I know very little of their early life here, only that they met in Glasgow when Father worked there for a time and that he brought her back here after they were married."

Mrs Robertson was busy dusting, but she stopped for a moment.

"Aye well, it wasn't easy for her," she said. "Brought up in a city and then coming to a wee place like Morach. I remember well the day they arrived. She was a pretty lass." Her eyes smiled. "You know, with her so slight now and that bonny colour, she looks more the girl she was then than she's ever done since. Aye, she was so happy. A bonny, bright lass until the gossip started. But your father soon put a stop to that. He was a kind man, your father, but he could be firm and he was always well respected in Morach. But it was too late by then. The damage had been done."

"What do you mean?" I said. "What damage? What gossip?"

She looked at me quickly. "Ah, don't mind me, Kirsty," she said. "My tongue runs away with me sometimes. I must be getting old."

I caught her arm as she turned away.

"Tell me," I said. "Surely I have a right to know?"

She hesitated. "It's a long time ago, Kirsty," she said. "What's the use of dragging up old gossip? It'll not help your mother."

I insisted. "Maybe not," I said. "But it'll maybe help me understand her better. What gossip?"

She sighed and crumpled the duster in her hand. I waited, breathless, then she seemed to make up her mind.

"It was to do with your father," she said. "He had been that set on one of the village girls. It was known in Morach they were walking out together. They'd even talked of posting the banns. Such a handsome couple they made! And then she threw him over or he threw her over. Some said one thing, some the other. But it was off to Glasgow for him and she was left here and there wasn't one among us who didn't think it a crying shame. But there you are, it happens. And so, when your father came back to Morach a full two years later, the tongues started wagging until he silenced them. It's a hard thing for a young bride to come to her husband's home and find she's not been his first choice." She was looking at me gently. "You see, Kirsty – it was nothing. But it made its mark on your mother. She couldn't forget that Morach knew more about her husband's past than she did."

I nodded. "Yes, I see that," I said. "It would mean a lot to Mother."

She turned to go but I stopped her. "Who was the girl, Mrs Robertson?" I asked. "The girl Father was to marry."

She looked at me for a long moment before saying, "It was Catriona MacLelland, Roddie's mother." Then she was gone.

I made no attempt to stop her. My mind was too busy trying to cope with the thoughts that flooded it. I thought of Mother and her dislike of Roddie. I thought of his illegitimacy. And suddenly, incredibly, I wondered if I had stumbled on what Mother had against Roddie. I recalled the rumours about his birth. His father was said to have been someone who had left the village, just as my father had done.

But could Mother really believe that Roddie was his child? I thought not. Not if she were reasonable. But love is not reasonable, I thought. Nor is jealousy – jealousy of her husband's first love, especially when that first love had died. She might persuade herself that it could not be true. But she would be haunted by doubts. She would never be entirely sure.

Roddie's mother had died by the time Father brought Mother to Morach as his wife. Mother would be too proud even to ask about Catriona MacLelland. But she would have heard the rumours surrounding Roddie's father. Her pride would have kept her silent on the subject, even with my father.

And then I caught myself up. I was letting my imagination run away with me. Of course she could not believe that! It was the fact that she had not been my father's first choice that rankled with her.

I saw so clearly how hard life had been for Mother in Morach, how she had needed to be different, how she had needed to keep her pride. Poor Mother! Roddie's grandmother had been right as always when she told me not to worry Mother, not to let her know how fond I was of Roddie. But perhaps I should tell her about Roddie and me. Then she would know she was wrong to suspect such things – if indeed she did suspect such a thing. After all, Roddie knew who his father was even if I did not. Mrs MacLelland had said so. Or perhaps I should tell Roddie what I was thinking. But I found the idea distasteful. He had only ever once mentioned his father. I could not bring that subject up with him even now with the understanding that was between us.

Not that Roddie and I had behaved any differently since that night on the moor. We hadn't. To all intents and purposes, nothing had changed between us. Indeed, if anything, I had seen and spoken to him less since then and there had been no repetition of that kiss. Sometimes I would even wonder if it had really happened. Then I would catch his eye and the understanding that was between us would seem solid once more. It was not exactly a secret but neither of us had mentioned it to anyone. It would upset Mother too much.

And so life at the castle went on much as usual and an onlooker would have seen no difference in the relationships between the four of us. Roddie still teased Charlotte and she continued to woo him after her own fashion. Richard still courted my favour, though not so assiduously as he had done, and I still fobbed him off. Perhaps Effie was right and he was growing tired of my constant refusals to be more than friends. One thing did comfort me at this time. That small nagging doubt I had, that Roddie had chosen me because I was "his kind" and Charlotte was not, was stilled. If he were more restrained than I would have wished, it was only to spare my mother pain.

I did not, however, have much time to brood on these matters for Mother grew weaker by the day and soon she no longer insisted on going up to the castle. I stayed at home with her, of course, talking when she felt able and trying to be cheerful. If anything, she was happier than I had ever seen her. We never mentioned her illness, merely spoke of it as a summer chill that would soon pass. We only came near the subject of death once. She was sitting propped up by the window, some sewing lying neglected in her lap, when she turned to me.

"Kirsty," she said, "there will come a time when you will make a life for yourself."

"That time comes for everyone," I said. "But I need not think of it just yet."

"I think the young laird is fond of you," she went on.

I dismissed her words as lightly as I could.

"Oh, Richard," I said. "He is not serious at all."

She looked at me very seriously. "And you?" she said.

I shrugged. "He's pleasant and amusing but. . ." I stopped. How could I explain why I should feel a need to be wary of Richard, why he frightened me a little?

"But what?" she said.

I hesitated, thinking of Richard's thoughtless treatment of Effie, of the way he could switch from laughing banter to intense anger in the space of a moment. "He's . . . moody," I said. "I don't feel entirely comfortable with him."

"It's just as well," she said. "You should stick to your own kind."

I almost smiled. She did not know how she echoed Roddie.

"There's no one else?" she was saying.

I felt myself flush as I looked at her.

"No," I lied. "There's no one else."

She sighed deeply, relief showing plainly in her face.

"There was a time", she said, "when I thought you were growing overfond of Roddie MacLelland."

I noticed again how she never called him Roddie, always Roddie MacLelland. Was it to remind herself that he was Catriona MacLelland's son? To persuade herself that he had nothing to do with my father? I found myself wondering again if she thought Roddie was my father's son. I could not help myself. I had lied about Roddie to protect her from hurt but, if my suspicion was correct, she was torturing herself for nothing.

"Would that be so bad?" I said.

She looked at me sharply, all the old alertness returning to her face.

"He is not for you, Kirsty," she said. "It would not be right."

"Why not, Mother?" I insisted. "He is a good man."

I watched her closely. I could do nothing unless she admitted what she suspected. I could not bring up such a dreadful suspicion. It would be unpardonable if I was mistaken.

Her cheeks grew brighter than ever and her breath became uneven as she took my hand in hers. I felt it burn in mine.

"Kirsty," she said, "it must not be. You have told me there is no one."

She was gasping for breath now and her hand was on fire. I leaned towards her, supporting her, and cursing myself for a fool to have upset her so.

"Hush, Mother! Hush!" I said. "You must not upset yourself."

Her eyes were bright and fevered.

"You will not marry him," she gasped. "You must promise me."

I looked at her, so ill, and I lied again. "No, Mother, I promise," I said. "Now, come to bed. You will make yourself ill."

I must have been near to hysteria for I almost laughed at my last words as I got her to bed. I stood by the window, listening to her breathing as she fell into a deep sleep.

Mrs MacLelland came that afternoon as she did every afternoon now and gave Mother her medicine. It was a strange thing but, though she could not bear my friendship with Roddie, she welcomed his grandmother and they would talk until she tired too much.

When Mrs MacLelland emerged from the bedroom she said, "She is not so well today, Kirsty. She seems upset."

I nodded. "It's my fault," I said. "I'm afraid I said something that worried her."

I was close to tears and she put her hand on my arm. I looked into those bright black eyes that saw so much.

"Roddie goes to Edinburgh tomorrow," she said. "He will be down at the boat this evening."

"To Edinburgh?" I said. "So soon?"

"He has been asked to do some tutoring," she said. "It is a great thing for him."

I was both glad for him and sad that he should leave Morach earlier than expected. But, as I walked down to the churchyard that evening, I persuaded myself to be happy at his getting on so well. He was just rowing into shore as I approached.

"You've been to the Druid Island," I said as he beached the boat.

"I wanted to go before I left," he said as he dragged *The Raven's Wing* up the shore.

"You should have waited," I said. "I would have gone with you."

"I wanted to go alone," he said. "I'll take you another time."

He seemed very serious and I teased him to bring the laughter back to his face.

"To walk round the Druid Stone?" I said.

Quite suddenly, he was standing over me, his hands on my arms, holding me so that I could not move.

"Don't say that, Kirsty," he said.

His face was strained, dark with some deep feeling I could not understand.

"What's the matter, Roddie?" I said. "I'm sorry. It was just a joke."

At once his grip relaxed and his arms went round me gently as the darkness cleared from his face and once more he was the Roddie I knew.

"No, no, it's I who should be sorry, Kirsty," he said. "Forgive me. But when you and I marry it will be properly. There will be no walking round the Druid Stone for us."

I cursed myself for a fool. What was it he had said to me years ago? That his mother and father had walked round the Druid Stone. That they had been married *after a fashion*.

At that moment a high, clear voice cut in and Charlotte said, "What a charming picture? The hero's farewell. I came to say goodbye, Roddie."

She was standing on the path behind us, the evening sun slanting through the trees and striking gleams of gold from her hair. Her gown was the colour of a mountain tarn and high on her cheekbones burned two bright spots of colour as red as the berries on the rowan trees around her.

Roddie let go of me so quickly, I almost stumbled as he said, "Good of you, Charlotte, but I would not leave Morach without saying my goodbyes."

Her eyes moved over me and sparked fire at him as she said, "So I see."

He bent casually to the boat to pick up the rope and walked towards her. With great care he tied the rope around a tree and turned to her.

"I will say my goodbye here then," he said, "since you have been so gracious as to come to me."

He took her by the shoulders and kissed her on the cheek. I saw her cling to him momentarily longer than he held her and then she said unsteadily, "And how many of those will you bestow on the girls of Morach before you go, Roddie?"

He laughed down at her. "I bestow them only where they give pleasure," he said.

"And they give pleasure to Kirsty?" she said.

Roddie smiled. "I should hope so," he said. "Kirsty and I are old friends."

"Indeed?" said Charlotte. "Only that?"

I saw a spark fly between them before she laughed and turned to lead the way back to the churchyard. I was about to speak, to ask Roddie why he had denied our love, but he put a finger gently on my lips and said softly, "Only trust me, Kirsty, and take care while I am away," and his lips brushed mine, feather-light, before he led me after Charlotte.

Her voice came floating back to us as we went. "I have a notion, Roddie, that you are not such a peasant as you make yourself out to be," she said. "Don't be surprised if I find myself making a visit to Edinburgh in the near future. I have a feeling you would be quite different there."

"Edinburgh drawings-rooms are hardly the natural haunts of poor students," said Roddie.

Charlotte looked back, her face bright with mischief under the gloom of the overhanging trees.

"But you are Roderick MacLelland," she said, "scholarship student and likely to be medallist of your year, the only one in history, it would appear, to be asked by Professor MacIvor to research for him before graduation."

I felt Roddie stiffen beside me. "How do you know that?" he said.

She laughed up at him, delighted with herself. "I had a letter from Annabelle MacIvor this morning," she said. "I knew her in Edinburgh last year. Her letter was full of the exciting young scholar who is coming to stay with them while her father writes his book. She says he is really quite handsome and has already made his mark on the academic world. Quite the pet of the scholastic community, in fact." Her eyes were triumphant as she finished. "She wonders if I am not bored to tears in Morach and asks me to come for a visit."

There was a moment's silence before he said with a smile, "I have no secrets."

"Not any more," she said, laughing up at him. "Your success is out. You've been hiding your light under the proverbial bushel."

I was totally confused. So this was his "tutoring"! I had thought Roddie just one of the many poor scholars who flocked to the universities of Scotland and now it seemed he was quite special and on his way to becoming a respected academic. He had not told me and, if he had not told me that, then what else had he not told me? Why had he said we were merely friends? What was between him and Charlotte? No one knew of the understanding between us. But surely that was for my mother's sake?

We had reached the village and Roddie would escort Charlotte back to the castle. It was only right. After all, had he himself not once said that her position demanded it? I looked at him as he took his leave of me. It would be some months before I would see him again and I could not ask him all the questions I wanted to, not with Charlotte there, tapping her foot impatiently in the background. His hands enveloped mine as I looked at him, all my dumb confusion showing in my eyes.

"Trust me, Kirsty," he said again and I nodded.

But I did not know what he meant, and then it was too late for he was gone. I listened for a moment to their voices receding into the night, Charlotte's light and bantering and his with its deep, amused replies. I felt tears on my cheeks as I pushed open the door but I could not tell their cause.

Chapter 11

As summer turned to autumn and the cold winds began to blow about Morach, it was as if Mother was in tune with the dying year. She grew frailer and soon it was impossible for me to go up to the castle at all. When I look back on it, it seems I moved through that time like a sleepwalker, neither knowing nor caring what went on around me, my whole being bent on making Mother's last weeks as comfortable as possible.

Scenes stand out to me like flashes of silver on a summer river – bright, clear and then gone as if they had no moment and no meaning. But they did have meaning. It was just that I was in no fit state to perceive it. And so I did not see the signs that heralded the dreadful end to that year but merely accepted them, not knowing, not caring.

The first of these occurred on one of my rare visits to Blair Morach. Charlotte had become weary of the castle and insisted that I come and entertain her, and I had complied. I had left Mother with Mrs MacLelland and, truth to tell, I was in need of a change from the sickroom.

I had grown pale and thinner and, as I walked up towards the gates, I drew in deep breaths of the crisp autumn air and felt guilty to be feeling so well and so free again.

Charlotte was nowhere to be found when I arrived, which was typical of her. I searched the house. It was oddly quiet. I thought I heard a sound as I left Charlotte's bedroom and turned up the stairs to the attic floor. As I mounted, the sound became unmistakable. Someone was sobbing and not quietly but with an uncontrollable abandon that masked my footsteps as I approached. Effie was lying full length on her narrow iron-framed bed, her thin shoulders shaking with the vehemence of her weeping. I went quickly to her and put a hand on her shoulder.

"Effie!" I said. "Why, whatever is wrong?"

At once she turned, her face blotched red and white from her crying. She sat up hurriedly, pushing her dishevelled hair out of her eyes.

"What are you doing here?" she said hoarsely. "You've no right to be here."

"I was looking for Charlotte," I said, "and I heard you crying. I couldn't just go away."

I sat down beside her but she turned away, burying her face in her hands.

"What's wrong, Effie?" I said again. "Something is troubling you deeply. Perhaps, if you tell me, I can help."

Her voice was muffled. "Nobody can help," she said. "Just go away and leave me alone."

Effie could be very stubborn. Perhaps later I might be able to talk to her. I rose to go and, as I did so, my foot kicked against something that was lying half under the bed. I stooped to pick it up. It was a small book in a green cloth cover and I frowned as I tried to remember where I had seen it before. As I held it loosely in my hands, it fell open and I caught sight of a chapter headed "Legends of the Druid Island". Then Effie rounded on me and snatched the book from me.

"And don't go snooping and prying either, Miss Clever," she said vindictively. "Keep out of my business."

I looked at her, sitting there amongst the rumpled bedclothes, her hair awry and her eyes red from crying. Her lips were curled in an ugly sneer but she looked somehow pitiful just the same.

I tried once again. "Effie," I said, "have you been frightening yourself with that silly book?"

Her face grew taut. "What do you mean? What do you know about it?" she asked.

I spread my hands. "I haven't read it," I said, "only looked over it once. But I know it's full of nonsense and old superstitions."

Her knuckles were white, she was clutching the book so tightly.

"And what would you know of old superstitions?" she said softly. Her voice sent a shiver down my spine. "You, who only half belong here," she finished.

I felt as if she had slapped me and suddenly I was angry.

"I know more than to upset myself over silly tales," I said shortly as I walked towards the door.

She was after me at once and I turned and faced her over the threshold.

"You wouldn't be so smug if you knew the 'silly tales'," she said. "Maybe you should have asked your father about them."

Before I could speak the door was slammed in my face and I heard the key turn. I hammered on the door.

"What do you mean, Effie?" I called. "Effie, open the door!"

But all I heard was a high-pitched giggle that turned to sobbing and nothing I could say would make her open the door.

I was still alternately pleading with her and hammering on the door when I heard Charlotte's voice.

"For goodness' sake, what's all the noise? Is that you, Kirsty?" she called.

I turned from the door and called back, "Yes, I came to find you – as requested."

"Well," she said, ignoring my last comment. "For pity's sake stop all that shouting and come down. I want to talk to you. What on earth are you doing up there anyway?"

Her voice faded as she made her way to her own room, obviously not interested enough to wait for an answer. I turned towards Effie's door once more. It was still firmly closed against me.

Once more I heard that high-pitched giggle and Effie's voice saying, "Run away now, Kirsty. The mistress of the house wants you."

Faintly Charlotte's voice floated up towards us, and I stamped my foot as I turned from the door and the sound of soft laughter.

Charlotte was waiting for me in her room surrounded by boxes and parcels which she was trying to open all at once.

"Do help, Kirsty," she said. "I've got such a lot to show you."

Obediently, I began untying string and opening parcels, and soon the room was draped with silks, satins and soft merino wool.

"What do you think?" she asked, her eyes shining as she looked at the lovely things. I fingered a length of pale yellow silk that shimmered and danced like water in sunlight.

"They're beautiful," I said truthfully. "But what are they for?"

Her face was bright with laughter as she said, "For my visit to Edinburgh. I had a letter from Annabelle this morning and I'm to go just as soon as I like. Of course I shall buy more clothes there, but I shall need a few things for when I first arrive."

I looked at the sea of materials before me. What Charlotte termed "a few things" would keep a Morach girl clothed for several years. But I did not say any of that for her words had struck me cold to the heart.

"Then you really are going to Edinburgh?" I said.

"Of course," she replied, throwing a length of blue merino over her shoulder and examining the effect in front of her looking-glass. "What do you think of this?"

I could hardly answer. The deep blue of the wool threw back the colour of her eyes and made a perfect foil for her hair. Golden hair, Roddie had called it. How could any man resist such beauty?

"It's lovely," I said.

She turned on me, a small frown between her eyes.

"You don't sound too enthusiastic," she said, and, mistaking my reaction, "What was all that shouting about?"

"Effie's upset," I said, glad that she had not picked on the real reason for my lack of enthusiasm. "She's locked herself in her room and she's crying her eyes out."

Charlotte looked at me incredulously. "Is that what's wrong with you?" she said. "Why you are ridiculous sometimes, Kirsty. Servants are always having hysterics. It's their station in life. They're forever being jilted by the footman, or the under-gardener or some such being."

I would have protested at such callousness. I was on the point of saying that if a man had made Effie unhappy it was more likely to be Richard than an under-gardener. But her next words drove the breath from my body.

"Do you think your mother could have these made up by the week after next?" she said casually. "I'd like to get away as soon as possible."

"No!" I said when I could speak again. "You know she can't, Charlotte. She's ill. How can you ask such a thing?"

Her pretty mouth pouted sullenly. "Oh, don't be so morbid, Kirsty," she said. "You know she loves these pretty things. If you won't ask her, I'll ask her myself. Besides, it'll take her mind off things, you wait and see. It'll probably do her more good than all old Mrs MacLelland's remedies put together."

I looked at her in disbelief, wondering if she really did believe what she was saying.

I thought that, on balance, she probably did. Charlotte seemed to have the gift of believing exactly what suited her. I turned on my heel and left her talking to the empty air. I could stand it no longer.

Perhaps it was the blaze of light beyond the gloom of the great hall or it could, I suppose, have been the tears that stood in my eyes, but I did not see Richard until I cannoned into him. His hands came out to my shoulders to steady me.

"Hey!" he said. "What's the rush? You nearly knocked me over."

I looked up at him, solid against the glancing light of the sunshine outside and I found myself leaning against him. At once his arms went round me and I felt his hand smooth my hair gently.

"Well, little bird, and what has upset you so much?" he said.

I shook my head, unable to speak, and he drew away from me slightly, tilting my chin to look into my face.

"Charlotte has done this, hasn't she?" he said. "Honestly, I could strangle that girl sometimes, cousin though she is! She didn't tell you she'd changed her plans and was going into Fort William this morning?"

I shook my head. "No, but it isn't that."

"Then what?" he said gently. Then his face changed. "Is it your mother?"

I nodded. It was true enough and I could not tell him of Charlotte's thoughtlessness.

He did not speak. What was there to say? He merely held me a moment longer before I gently released myself.

"Thank you, Richard," I said.

He shrugged, "For what?"

"For being kind," I answered.

At once his face was grave as he said, "With you, Kirsty, I feel I could always be kind. You would be the saving of me."

I smiled, not wanting to take him seriously.

"Save you from what?" I asked lightly.

"From myself," he replied, still as grave.

I laughed it off then.

"No one can do that for another person," I said.

He looked at me for a long moment, then shrugged again and I was relieved to see a lightening of his expression.

"You're right, of course," he said. "We make our own destiny."

His words struck a chord and I said, "Oh Richard, Effie has got hold of that book about Morach and she seems to have frightened herself out of her wits. You know the book – the one with all those dreadful old superstitions in it."

He had started to turn away but my words stopped him and he turned back slowly.

"Book?" he said.

"The one you showed me in the library long ago," I said. "About the Druid Island and ancient customs."

"Oh, that book," he said, clearly puzzled. "But what is Effie doing with it?"

"Perhaps you left it lying around," I said.

He made a face. "Perhaps," he said. "I haven't seen it for ages but I rather had the impression Roddie found it interesting." He smiled at me. "Effie's a silly girl and you're not to worry yourself on her account."

I smiled back. "I won't," I said. "But I don't think that book is doing her any good."

"I'll have a word with her," he said and I left it at that, glad at any rate that he knew. Effie would talk to him even if she wouldn't talk to me.

I made my way, as always when I needed to think, down to the churchyard and through the lych-gate. And, as I sat watching the sun on the oaks of The Druid Island, I wondered what Roddie had found so interesting about that book. For all he disliked it, he was as fascinated by the island as I was and I found myself wishing he had taken me on that final trip out to it before he went away. Then I found myself thinking of his anger when I said I would walk round the Druid Stone with him. I felt myself tense as I thought of it. I wished I had. I wished I had walked round the Druid Stone with him for then he would be safe from Charlotte and her beauty, and her drawing-room ways.

I should have expected it, I suppose, but still it came as a shock to me when I got back to the cottage and opened the door on a flood of colour: Charlotte's materials. I looked at my mother propped up in a chair by the window, her face more flushed than ever and her eyes unnaturally bright as she looked up from the pale yellow silk she was stitching.

"Mother, what are you doing out of bed?" I said, my voice sharper than I had intended.

"Now, don't scold, Kirsty," she said excitedly. "Miss Charlotte is going to Edinburgh to visit a friend and brought me her patterns and materials to be made up. She came down to the cottage herself, you know, and we had quite a little chat. She's told me exactly what she wants and says she wouldn't for the world want me to tire myself, but my sewing is so good she wouldn't dream of going to anyone else. Isn't that so, Mrs MacLelland?" And she turned, breathless, to Roddie's grandmother who was bent over the table cutting out the rest of the pattern.

"That's what she said," said Mrs MacLelland and, as her eyes met mine, I stifled the protest that rose to my lips. "She seems very set on having them just right for this visit to Edinburgh, though what she needs with new clothes and her with enough things up there to dress the women of Morach three times over, I don't know."

"Oh, come now, Mrs MacLelland!" protested my mother. "A young woman like that needs to be in the fashion and they say Edinburgh is nearly as stylish as London these days."

Mother talked on of how kind Charlotte had been to call herself and not just send the things down, of how pretty she was and of how she loved to make up such wonderful materials, while Mrs MacLelland cut and pinned and made everything ready for her to sew.

But I noticed that her needle did not fly as quickly as it had done and the flush in her cheeks died to a weary pallor before she had set the work aside. She lay back in her chair at last and fell asleep. Mrs MacLelland stopped me before I could say a word.

"Now, who's to say it's not good for her?" she said.

"How can you say that?" I asked. "Why, she's ill!"

"Aye, and there's no betterment for her, but at least she's being useful, doing something she wants to do. It isn't as if she's hemming sheets. You heard her talk of how it took her back to her days in Glasgow when she met your father. She loves this work."

"But Charlotte's only using her!" I said, frustrated.

"Does it matter, Kirsty," Mrs MacLelland said, "if it makes her happy?"

"But it's not right, it's not fair!" I said.

She smiled then. "There you go again," she said. "And who ever said life was fair? Just look at her eyes when she's handling that silk. She's as happy as a lintie, Kirsty, and you must not take that away from her."

I looked at Mrs MacLelland dumbly, everything in me wanting to protest. But I knew she was right.

"She won't get them finished in time on her own," I said.

Again the black eyes looked into mine. "She's not on her own," she said.

My eyes fell before hers and I studied the toes of my shoes mutinously. She did not know what she was asking. Her old, lined hand touched mine briefly.

"Don't set yourself up in judgement, lass," she said.

I don't know how long I stood there. I heard the door open softly, felt the cool of the evening air before it closed again, leaving only the sounds of the clock on the mantelshelf and the soft breathing of my mother asleep in her chair. And when I moved, it was to take the yellow silk from my mother's lap and sit down by the light of the lamp.

That was how I came to sew Charlotte's gowns far into the night, every night for more than a week, so that Mother might not be overstrained and Charlotte would have her Edinburgh gowns with which to dazzle Roddie.

I wondered if he would be dazzled. She was beautiful enough and determined enough to overcome any opposition that might be put in her way. Each to their own. Would the Laird feel that too? But Charlotte would have her way no matter what the Laird said.

I was more and more convinced that she really loved Roddie despite what he said. She had once called him a peasant but she did not think of him as such any longer. And nor, it seemed, was he thought of in that way in Edinburgh. Roddie was headed for great things. And Charlotte, I was sure, wanted to be at his side. He was gone far away from me, and Charlotte would be with him. How could I compete with that?

Chapter 12

By the time Charlotte was due to leave, all her gowns were ready. Mother was so pleased as she helped me pack them into the trunk that had been sent down from the castle. I was no longer angry about it and, when Charlotte herself stopped by on her way to Edinburgh and gave Mother a pretty cameo brooch, she flushed bright with pleasure.

"So kind, Miss Charlotte, but really there was no need," said Mother.

"Nonsense," said Charlotte. "You are easily the best seamstress in the Highlands and the gowns are beautiful."

She was wearing the blue merino travelling dress with a small fur hat and muff and fur-trimmed cape, and even I got a perverse pleasure out of seeing our handiwork so well displayed. She put a gloved hand on my arm and drew me outside. There was an edge to the air now, and the trees down by the loch were beginning to shed their green and take on the browns and russets of autumn.

"Well, Kirsty," she said. "Shall I give Roddie your love?"

"You seem quite certain of seeing him," I replied.

She laughed. "Oh, I intend to see a great deal of Mr MacLelland," she said. "After all I shall be living in the house of his patron."

She looked so confident, so sure of herself. Then she said, "Of course I am not without competition," and my heart gave a little leap.

I looked into her eyes, so blue and guileless above the fur at her throat.

"Competition?" I said as calmly as I could.

She tweaked at her cape again. "Yes. It seems, from her letters, that Annabelle is also quite stricken with him. But I don't think I need to worry too much about that, do you?"

I found myself feeling quite sorry for the unknown Annabelle and I smiled at myself. With such a picture of beauty before me I should be feeling sorry for myself!

She took a step towards the waiting carriage.

"I'll give him your love then, shall I?" she said again and I had no idea whether there was more than just idle chatter in her reference to Annabelle.

"Tell him I shall see him at Hallowmas," I said carefully.

"Hallowmas?" she repeated.

"It's a Scottish quarter day," I explained. "The University will be on holiday and he will come home then."

She smiled at me then and I knew that she was deliberately taunting me.

"He may find Edinburgh more to his taste," she said.

Our eyes met and for a moment we were locked in silent battle before I said with more confidence than I felt, "He will come home."

She shrugged and the moment was gone.

"We shall see, Kirsty," she said. "Goodbye!"

I watched the carriage until it turned a bend in the road and was lost to view. Then I went back into the cottage.

Mother was sitting in her chair by the window where I had left her, but now her skin was ashen and her breath coming in short gasps. I managed to get her to bed before going for Mrs MacLelland, but there was little we could do. It was as if she had used up all her remaining strength in these last two weeks. We sat with her all night, taking turns at her bedside, cooling her fevered forehead with damp cloths.

Once and only once I said, "I should send for the doctor."

But Roddie's grandmother shook her head and I did not suggest it again. It had been said more in hope than anything else, for even I could see that doctors were no good to my mother any more. She was delirious, wandering in a world of her imagination and muttering words I could barely understand. I heard over and over my father's name.

It was towards dawn, as the first faint lightening of the sky made the candles burn more weakly, when Mother suddenly opened her eyes and looked quite calmly into mine.

"You are a good girl, Kirsty," she said. "Your father would be proud of you and I have always loved you dearly."

Then her eyes closed for the last time and a small sigh escaped her lips before her head fell sideways on the pillow. It was the first time she had told me she loved me.

I did not cry. Not then, nor at the funeral. But I did everything that Mrs MacLelland told me and marvelled at how strange life was. As I walked down to the church with the women of the village, I looked at the procession of men in front of me and wanted to run through them, to shout in their faces, "Why could you not have been like this while she was alive?"

But I knew in my heart that they had tried. Still, it was strange that in death she had become more a part of the village than she had been in life. As was the custom, all the men of Morach had turned out in their sober Sunday black, carrying the coffin six by six down through the village to the church. Every man had his turn, every man in Morach bore her burden through the village while the women walked behind.

A few leaves drifted across the grass as we emerged from the service and, as the women turned back towards the village, leaving the men to the burial, the smell of new dug earth came faintly to me. I was reminded of the smell of fresh dug peats on the moor and I wished that Roddie were here that I might weep.

I murmured the usual thanks to the mourners who offered sympathy, and later I handed the tea, offered the whisky and pressed the good things the women had brought to the house on my guests. But they did not stay long and soon only the Laird and Richard were left in our tiny parlour.

The Laird took my hand gently in his. "You are coming to Blair Morach this very night," he said. "I would not like to think of you here alone."

I thought of protesting but found that I did not care where I was, so I merely nodded my head and gathered my things together to take up to the castle. Richard shouldered the box that contained my few possessions and, as I saw him silhouetted against the open doorway, the old wooden box that my father had made on his shoulders, I felt hysteria rising in me and heard wild laughter ring through the cottage. It was such a parody of the funeral procession.

The slap was meant kindly. I put my hand to my cheek, shaking uncontrollably. I realized that the laughter had been mine. I looked at the Laird, shocked out of my hysteria by the blow, and then the tears came and it was comforting to weep in his arms, for he had been a friend to my father. When the sobbing had ceased I found that I was once more in command of myself, as I had not been these last few days. Richard had gone, presumably sent up to the castle with my things. I looked around the little cottage which had been my only home.

"You're right," I said. "I cannot stay here. Not at the moment anyway."

So the Laird took my arm and together we walked up to the gates of Blair Morach and passed through them. I gave myself into his keeping until such time as Roddie would come home.

It was during those weeks of autumn that I really came to know the Laird, to admire and respect him. I was waiting for Hallowmas and Roddie's homecoming and I did not think of my future. I merely lived each day as it came until I found one morning, quite unexpectedly, that I was happy. I woke to find my bedroom window patterned with frost and the grass of the castle parkland sparkled like jewels in the morning sun. The frost had come early this year. For the first time in many weeks I was glad to be alive, with a joy that was almost fierce in its intensity.

I dressed quickly in my warmest things and slipped out of the castle before breakfast. I wanted to be up on the moor, as close to the sky as I could get, and to look down on Morach as it woke to a new day. I climbed so quickly that I did not feel the cold, even when I reached the top of the hill and stood there looking at the land spread out before me. The ground was hard as iron beneath my feet and my stout boots crunched as I walked. It was unusual weather, for there were still two weeks till Hallowmas and I hugged myself as I thought of it. Two weeks and Roddie would be home! Two weeks and I could once again think of the future. The ground crackled behind me and I whirled round to find Richard approaching, his long strides covering the ground in an easy lope. The wind whipped my hair across my face and I laughed as I pulled it back.

"Why, Richard!" I said. "You look as if you belong here."

He was level with me now and he stopped. "And why should I not?" he said. "Am I not the young laird?"

I laughed again at his attempt at the idiom of the village.

"What are you doing up here so early?" I asked.

He shrugged. "Same as you, I expect," he said. He took a deep breath of the frosty air. "I often come up here before breakfast," he went on. "Up here I feel free, untrammelled. It's a good place to think."

"And what do you think about?" I said and wished I had not, as I saw his eyes shadow.

"Of you usually," he replied.

I turned away, not wanting to continue the conversation. "Richard, you mustn't," I began. But his hands were on my shoulders, swinging me round so that I was forced to look at him.

"It's Roddie, isn't it?" he said. "You can't think of anyone but him. I've always known it, Kirsty, even before you did. You didn't realize it until Charlotte started taking an interest in him."

I tried to free myself but he held me fast.

"If it weren't for him you could care for me," he said. "You know you could. You almost did before. Deny it, Kirsty! Deny it!"

I couldn't deny it. At least I couldn't deny that I was in love with Roddie, or that once I had been attracted to Richard. I had *almost* cared for him at one time. But he was wrong when he said that it was Roddie that kept me from loving him. I knew now that something in Richard himself did that – an unsteadiness that I had glimpsed from time to time and that made me wary of him. I was silent. What good would it do to tell him that? Better to let him think that it was Roddie. Surely that would be better for his pride.

Richard was not looking at me. There was a faraway look in his eyes as he let me go and swung away down the hill, and I shivered as I watched him go. It was cold up there on the exposed hill. I hugged myself for warmth. What I needed was breakfast.

There was a letter waiting for me when I got back to the castle. It was from Charlotte. She was coming home for Hallowmas. I had not heard from Roddie apart from a brief note, full of sympathy for me on my mother's death. For such a scholar, he was not a great correspondent. I sat staring at Charlotte's letter, wishing it told me more. But it was full of nonsense about soirées and theatres and balls at the Assembly Rooms and then, tacked on at the end, ". . .Roddie and I will travel together of course. And you need not worry about propriety, Miss Goody Two Shoes. My maid will be with us."

I looked at the two words that leapt out of the page at me. *Of course!* I didn't want to think what that meant. I looked across at the

Laird. We were alone at the breakfast table for Richard had not yet returned.

"I've had a letter from Charlotte," I said.

He looked up from his own correspondence. "So have I," he said. "She wants me to give a ball at Hallowmas."

I smiled, "She seems to have enjoyed Edinburgh," I said. "She'll miss the gaiety when she comes home. A ball would be a nice idea. It's a long time since Hallowmas was celebrated at the castle though we always have a ceilidh in the village."

He frowned. He had been looking tired recently. "Yes, I expect you're right," he said. "There isn't much to keep a young person here, Kirsty."

"I'm happy in Morach," I said.

He smiled across the table at me. "Indeed you are and thank the Lord for it. It's a great pleasure for me to have you about the place, Kirsty. But you haven't known anything different, not like Charlotte and Richard."

And not like Roddie, I added to myself, but the Laird was speaking again.

"I worry about Richard," he said. "He seems to take himself off so much, often for nearly a whole day at a time, and he doesn't have the interest in the estate that I'd hoped for." He was speaking almost to himself now. "Maybe I did the wrong thing bringing him back here," he said. "But what else could I do? After that business at Oxford. . ." His voice trailed away and I doubt if he knew I was even there.

"You mean the accident?" I said.

He came to himself with a start. "Accident?" he said. "Yes, it was an accident, wasn't it? Just foolish student tricks. He's young yet."

I wondered then whether that incident had been more than an accident. I remember Charlotte's words when Roddie was hurt. "Not again!" Was it recklessness and not just carelessness that caused these "accidents"? I would have liked to pursue the subject for I too had noticed that Richard's moods were getting more unpredictable and, if I knew why, perhaps I could help. Was Richard able to control his moods or did the moods control him? But I didn't get the chance to broach the subject. The Laird stood up briskly.

"Well, I suppose we'd better get this ball organized, Kirsty," he said. "Let's make it a really splendid occasion. It'll be good for all of us."

I smiled. "I always loved Hallowmas when I was a child," I said. "Dressing up and wearing masks and going from house to house with turnip lanterns."

He laughed. "When you were a child, Kirsty?" he repeated. "Why, you're hardly more than that now!"

164

"I'm nineteen," I said. "That isn't a child."

Again the strained look returned. "No," he said, "and more's the pity. If only our children could stay children for ever. But then, that's a daft thing to say, isn't it?"

I didn't reply and he went on. "Richard is almost twenty-one," he said, "but he shows no sign of settling to anything – certainly not the estate. And look at Roddie! Only a year older and with none of Richard's advantages and yet he's already making a name for himself in Edinburgh." He shook his head.

"Roddie's different," I said. "He's always had to work. He's used to it."

"I suppose so," said the Laird.

"My father always said Roddie would get on," I said. "He used to say he had come of good stock."

The Laird smiled at me. "Your father!" he said. "Now, there's a man I was proud to know. I only wish I could have seen him again and made my peace with him."

I was immediately interested. "You quarrelled?"

"Just before he left for Glasgow," the Laird said.

"What did you quarrel about?" I asked.

He looked all at once twenty years younger.

"A girl," he said. "What else do young men quarrel about?"

I don't know quite why I was so sure. "It was about Catriona MacLelland, wasn't it?" I said.

He looked at me in surprise. "Now, how did you know?" he said.

I hesitated. "I knew he was in love with her years ago," I said.

"Aye, she was a bonny lass," the Laird said, "the bonniest in Morach. But it was a long time ago, Kirsty, and I've often thought if I hadn't been so stupid things might have gone better for me. It was a sad business, a bad business."

I waited, silent, for him to continue. But he turned from the table. "Let's not drag up past history," he said. "It's a bad idea. Come now, we must get this ball sorted out."

I threw myself into the preparations for the ball with a will. Even Richard seemed diverted by the prospect and insisted that everyone should come in fancy dress. I agreed to all his plans, for it was good to see him happy again, full of his usual jokes and nonsense.

The whole house was alive with the sounds and scents of cleaning and polishing, and the great hall began to glow with the warm colours of gorse and evergreen as branches were hung on the walls. The only sour note was struck by Effie, who had grown more and more sullen recently. I was stricken by remorse when I realized that I had not found out what had been troubling her the day Charlotte announced she was going to Edinburgh.

She came into the large dining-room as Richard and I were hanging hawthorn from the chandeliers. I was perched on a ladder, tying ribbons of scarlet and gold to the hanging branches and laughing down at Richard, when she came in with a loaded tray of glasses. It was the afternoon of the ball and Charlotte was expected home any moment. I smiled down at Effie, then noticed how pale and tired she looked.

"Why, Effie! You don't look at all well," I said. "Richard, take the tray from her. She doesn't look fit to carry it."

"I'm fit enough," said Effie shortly. But Richard moved forward and relieved her of the tray.

"And are you going to the ceilidh in the village tonight, Effie?" I asked.

She pushed a straggling lock of hair off her forehead. "I might," she said, "once I get finished here."

I smiled. "You'll be finished early enough," I said. "I've made sure of that."

The ceilidh didn't start until an hour before midnight and went on until the early hours, unlike the more seemly entertainment at the castle that was due to finish around the witching hour.

"Well, ma'am, I'm sure I'm very grateful to you for that," said Effie spitefully, and I felt my cheeks flame.

"Effie!" Richard said and his voice was like the crack of a whip.

She rounded on him. "Well, what do you expect and her acting the lady all over the place?" she said.

"That's enough," Richard replied.

She looked at him for a moment, then said in a more subdued voice, "Aye, you're right, it's enough."

At that moment there was the sound of voices in the hall and the door burst open to reveal Charlotte, radiant in an obviously new and expensive cherry-red travelling dress. She clapped her hands as she caught sight of the decorations.

"Oh, how wonderful!" she said. "I was afraid you wouldn't have arranged it."

"How could we refuse?" I said wryly but she didn't hear me. She was already engaged in conversation with Richard about the dreadful state of the roads and how exhausted she was.

"Of course, Roddie was simply marvellous," she was saying. "I just couldn't have managed without him." My hand closed unconsciously on a branch of hawthorn and I winced as it came in contact with the sharp barbs.

"Is Roddie here?" I asked.

She looked up at me. "Really, Kirsty," she said. "You look a perfect hoyden up there with your hair coming down and your face all red. Couldn't Richard do that?"

"I don't have the artistic touch," Richard said, smiling as he stretched up his arms to me and lifted me down from the ladder.

Charlotte's eyes flashed and she turned to Effie, but Effie was looking at Richard and me as we stood, his arms still round my waist. Charlotte had to say Effie's name twice before she took her eyes off us. She looked away, but not before I had seen the look in her eyes – a look compounded of love, jealousy and desperation. I wondered if Richard knew exactly how Effie felt about him. I wondered also just what kind of encouragement he had been giving her. He was so careless of her feelings.

"Go and run me a bath for goodness' sake, Effie!" Charlotte said. "I feel I've got half of Scotland on me."

Effie went without a word and Charlotte raised her eyes.

"You know, I sometimes wonder if that girl is half-witted," she said. "I caught her brewing up the most nauseating concoction of herbs and things just before I went away. She would have drunk it too if I hadn't insisted she throw it away."

My attention was immediately caught. "What kind of concoction?" I said. "What was it for?"

She lifted her hands to remove her hat. "How would I know?" she said. "Maybe she's a witch like Roddie's grandmother. It's the right time for it anyway – the night in the year when all the ghosties and ghoulies come out. Roddie was telling me all about your heathen customs up here. You really are a bloodthirsty lot, Kirsty."

"Hallowmas has always been celebrated in Scotland," I said. "It's one of the big days of the year for us, though I don't know that the minister really approves. Still, he shuts his door and lets the village get on with it. There's no harm in it."

"Not like there used to be", said Richard in bloodcurdling tones, "in the old days!"

I laughed. "You've been listening to too many stories," I said. "Morach is a very respectable place."

"It may be now," he went on, "but scratch the surface and you come across all sorts of beliefs that survive still."

Into my mind flashed the picture of Effie brewing up her "nauseating concoction" and the little green book full of old legends of Morach. I wondered again what that brew had been for – some kind of love potion perhaps? Or a remedy for something a lot more worrying? But then Charlotte spoke.

"Come upstairs at once, Kirsty," she said. "You must see my gown. Richard wrote that it was to be fancy dress and I got the most wonderful little woman in Edinburgh to make it for me." She turned as she said it, then paused as if her own words had reminded her. "Oh, I'm so sorry about your mother, Kirsty!" she said. Then, as I murmured something, she swept from the room in her usual fashion.

Richard smiled at me sympathetically. "She'll never be any different," he said.

"I don't suppose she will," I replied, soothed by his concern. He really could be the kindest person sometimes.

"Let me go and have a word with her before you go up," he said.

"Don't fuss, Richard," I said.

He laughed. "It's just this overwhelming urge I have to protect you," he said. But his eyes belied the lightness of his voice as he said, "I'd do anything for you, Kirsty."

It was some little time before I heard him come down, but he did not return to the dining-room and a few moments later I saw him through the window striding out towards the main gates. He turned once to look back at the house and I drew back from the window as I saw the expression on his face. I could not describe it even to myself, but it seemed to be like the face of someone who has been to the edge of darkness and back again. What on earth had happened to make him look like that? Surely not his conversation with Charlotte? I shook my head free of such nonsense. Charlotte would be waiting for me.

Chapter 13

Charlotte was in her small dressing-room, immersed in her bath, when I went up.

"Is that you, Kirsty?" she called. "I'll be out in a minute. The gown is on the bed."

There was a roaring fire in the grate but the lamps had not yet been lit and the late afternoon light was fading. I looked at Charlottes gown, a deceptively simple affair of white silk and tartan. I had guessed even before she said it.

"Flora MacDonald," she called. "Very Scottish, very romantic. Rescuing Bonnie Prince Charlie! What do you think?"

I smiled. "You'll look lovely," I said.

She entered the bedroom rosy and flushed from her bath, and pulling on a peignoir as she came. Her hair lay like a shining cloud around her shoulders. She would look lovely in rags.

She picked up a fold of the gown and let it fall. "Of course, it's silk," she said. "I didn't want to take the homespun look too far."

"Of course," I repeated, suppressing a smile. Flora MacDonald had been no peasant. She had come from a very good family.

Charlotte looked at me sharply. "What are you going as?" she asked.

I hesitated. It sounded too ridiculous but no one knew yet and, now that someone had asked, I felt myself too shy to say. It had seemed such a wonderfully romantic idea at the time and Roddie would be home.

"My mother had some materials in the cottage," I said. "I made up a gown from them."

"Oh, bits and pieces," she said dismissively. "If you'd said, I'd have brought you something from Edinburgh."

"I shall do well enough," I said.

"I dare say you will," she said, unconcerned. "Roddie refused to wear a disguise. He's coming in Highland dress which I said was fancy enough anyway."

I could imagine his face at that, or at least I thought I could.

"He'll be going to the ceilidh in the village afterwards," I said.

She looked at me in surprise. "Why on earth would he do that? He's coming here."

"He always goes to the ceilidh," I said. "The whole village does. The ball is for the gentry."

"Don't be ridiculous, Kirsty!" Charlotte said. "You're coming to the ball, aren't you?"

I flushed. "I don't have a home in the village any longer," I said.

"No," she said. "You don't, do you?"

She picked up a hairbrush from her dressing-table and sat down before her looking-glass, brushing her hair in long, sweeping strokes.

"Sit down, Kirsty," she said. "I've got something to say to you."

All at once my heart felt like lead within me.

"Roddie and I have been seeing a great deal of each other in Edinburgh," she said, and the lead turned cold as ice.

I sat down on the edge of her bed and watched, fascinated by the movement of the brush through her hair.

"We have grown fond of each other," she went on. "I think being away from Morach has helped us see each other differently. He is not the Morach crofter he appears to be, you know, Kirsty. In Edinburgh he is respected as a clever and cultured young man. Really, you would not recognize him there. And I am quite certain that he would be equally well regarded in London."

She paused and looked at me in the mirror, but the light was fading fast and I could hardly see the colour of her eyes. They seemed darker somehow. My mouth was dry and I could not speak. I saw her mouth tighten as she reached across her dressing-table and her face seemed very pale. She lit the candles in the sconces at the sides of her looking-glass. I was glad, for, while it illuminated her, it left me in shadow. Once again she picked up her brush and began to brush her hair.

The candles flickered at her movement and caught the gold of her hair in their radiance. She sat there in her pool of light and began to speak again as I watched from the shadows.

"There is one problem," she said. "He tells me there is some understanding between you and him. Oh, not a formal engagement – nothing as definite as that. But he says that he has given you to understand that he cares for you. Now, don't mistake me, Kirsty. He does care for you very much indeed. He knew that your mother did not have long to live and that you would be on your own. He also recognizes a great debt to your father, who was always kind to him and encouraged him in his ambition."

The brush stopped and she clasped it before her, gazing at me in the mirror, her eyes very wide and dark.

"Did you never wonder why your father was so kind to him, Kirsty?" she said.

I looked at her image in the mirror. She seemed unreal.

"Father liked Roddie," I said. "They got on well together."

"And so they should," she continued. "Fathers and sons often do."

It was as if the looking-glass shattered into fragments before my eyes. Her image became indistinct and there was a roaring in my ears.

"No!" I said. "That is not true!"

I heard her voice go inexorably on.

"Your father was also his father," she said. "No one was certain at the time, for he went off to Glasgow not knowing that Catriona MacLelland was pregnant and she would never tell anyone who Roddie's father was. Then, when your father came back to Morach, married and with a child, after Catriona had died, he went a little mad for a while. I expect it was hard on your mother. You see, he had cut himself off from Morach altogether while he was in Glasgow. He did not know he had a son. But when he returned, he did all he could for the boy. Of course no one in Morach referred to it openly, though I expect even you have heard rumours. It must have been difficult for your mother."

I could not see her. I could not see anything for the black mist that engulfed me. Someone was shaking me, calling my name. The mist cleared and I looked up. Charlotte was bending over me, her hair falling forward over my face so that I seemed caught in a golden net.

"It isn't true," I whispered. "It cannot be true. Roddie would never have said the things he did..."

Her face grew very still and she said, "Roddie does not know and you must never tell him."

"Then how do you know?" I said.

Her eyes dropped and then she raised them to mine. She was very close to me and I could see green flecks in the blue of her eyes that I had not noticed before.

"My uncle was friend to your father at that time," she said. "He also was in love with Catriona MacLelland. Most unsuitable, of course, and it's a well-kept secret in the family that he actually wanted to marry her. Naturally it was impossible, especially when she became pregnant by another man. You do see that, don't you?"

I nodded but I felt it hardly mattered. Mother had been right in her suspicions and I had been wrong to dismiss them as imaginings.

"But how could Roddie not know?" I said.

She laughed scornfully. "He has lived with his grandmother," she said.

I was about to protest when her last words sank in. His grandmother, who saw everything and bent everyone to her will. In a way Charlotte's joke about her being a witch was no joke at all. I remembered her telling me that Roddie knew who is father was. But he couldn't have known. His grandmother must have made up some story to satisfy his questions. He would believe her before he would believe village gossip.

"And your father was a much respected man," said Charlotte. "He silenced the gossip – for your mother's sake."

Not soon enough, I thought. Mother must have heard that gossip when she first came to Morach. But everything in me protested. . .

"I cannot believe it," I said.

Charlotte drew away from me. "Then ask someone else," she said.

She moved and, behind her, a figure stood, blurred against the outline of the dressing-room doorway.

"It's true enough, Miss High and Mighty," Effie said. "You should have asked your mother. Losh, Kirsty, your face is just a picture!"

I recalled that it was Effie's mother who had first alerted me to my mother's suspicions.

"That's all now, Effie," Charlotte said. "You may go."

Effie would have spoken further, but Charlotte motioned her to leave the room.

"She was there all the time?" I said.

"She passes for a lady's maid," said Charlotte.

I felt crushed, as if a great weight had been thrust upon me and I could not bear it.

"I must go," I said.

Her hand reached out and grasped my wrist. "Not until you have promised to say nothing of this to Roddie," she said.

I almost laughed. "What's the point in that?" I said. "If Effie is talking about it then soon everyone will know."

Charlotte's grip tightened, hurting me. "Effie will not tell anyone. I will see to that. You will promise me. This could destroy Roddie – to know the whole village has been laughing up its sleeve at him for years."

I nodded. She was right. It could do no good and, to tell the truth, I could not bear the thought of saying such things to him.

"You need not worry," I said. "I shall free him of his promise tonight and I shall not tell him the truth."

I shall lie, Mrs MacLelland, I thought. I shall lie because it will hurt less – just as you must have lied to him.

Charlotte let me go then and I made my way to my own room. It was strange that I was so calm. I could not understand it.

Chapter 14

I sat in my room for a long time, going over in my mind again and again what Charlotte had told me. My mother's face rose before my eyes and I wept. How she must have suffered! At last I raised my head. It was time to dress for the ball. I gazed at my face in the looking-glass. It was just the same. How strange! I thought. How can I look no different when my life has been shattered? I lifted my chin. I would release Roddie from his promises. He would be glad of it if he was in love with Charlotte. For a moment my courage failed. Would I have the strength to tell him I no longer cared for him?

I dressed carefully, calmly, with no sense of hurry. Soon I would be seeing Roddie. I must make him believe that I no longer loved him. And I must not love him, not now. I would think about that later. For the moment I would concentrate all my will on my pretence.

I dropped the gown I had made over my head and fastened it up, trying all the while not to remember all the love and happiness that had gone into the making of it for his home-coming. I unpinned my hair and let it fell loosely around my shoulders, brushing it into shining waves, and only when I had finished did I look in my mirror.

Before me stood a creature of myth and legend. The gown fell in long, drifting folds to my feet, the sea-green silk chiffon floating over an underdress of ivory-coloured taffeta. My skin was pale and luminous in the candlelight and the soft fall of the gown emphasized my slenderness. My hair, the colour of a raven's wing, rippled almost to my waist, shining with light from the ivory of the underdress, and my eyes were huge and dark with sorrow. Never again would I look so lovely or so sad. I marvelled that scraps saved by my mother from her days as a seamstress in Glasgow could have been transformed into something so beautiful. As I moved, the dress shimmered like moonlight on water. That's what I was tonight – a creature of moonlight, a sea creature for All Hallows' Eve.

I walked calmly down the stairs to the great hall. Guests had already started to arrive. I saw Charlotte, sparkling in white and the glowing colours of her plaid, greet them as they came in. All the great houses and some of the lesser ones of the county had been invited. Soon Roddie would walk through those great double doors and I would have to meet his eyes and lie.

I was standing at the foot of the stairs, quite still, when I heard footsteps behind me and turned to see Richard coming down the staircase. His eyes travelled over my face and my gown and I saw him draw in his breath. Then he put his arm under my elbow and, without speaking, led me to the door of the library, away from the arriving guests.

He pushed open the door and ushered me in. I went obediently, glad of the support of his arm. No candles or lamps burned here, but the curtains had not been drawn and the light of the frosty moon bathed the room. He turned as I came in and his face told me I was lovely.

"Kirsty," he said, "I cannot stand this any longer. I love you. I want to marry you." He shook his head slowly. "If you only knew how much I love you! I would do anything for you. I would do anything to make you love me. And you are so unhappy."

I looked at him, standing there watching me, his fair hair silvered by the moonlight flooding through the windows. At that moment he seemed so vulnerable, and he cared so much for me! He made to speak again but I moved towards him and put out my hand. He seized it in his own and drew me towards him. I went, unresisting, glad to have his warm arms around me, to have his warm breath on my cheek. I felt so cold.

"Marry me, Kirsty," he said. "I swear I will make you happy. Only, marry me."

I looked up at him. Why not? I thought. At least I could make Richard happy. Why not?

"Perhaps," I said. "In time. But you must give me time, Richard."

A flame leapt behind his eyes and he searched my face. Then he bent his head to mine.

"Kirsty!" he said before he kissed me.

His lips felt cold on mine but perhaps that was due to the chill I now seemed to carry with me. He did not seem dissatisfied however and, thankfully, he did not ask any questions.

He took my arm and led me out to the hall. It was a pity that Roddie chose just that moment to arrive, for Richard must have felt the swift flicker of fire that ran through my body. But he said nothing, merely held my arm a little more firmly as Roddie approached us.

"Kirsty!" he said, holding out his hands to me, and I could have drowned in the love and warmth that was in his eyes. Charlotte was immediately at his shoulder, watchful of my response.

"Roddie!" I replied. "How lovely to see you."

My voice was calm and cool and I saw his eyes narrow slightly as he checked his progress towards me.

"You and Charlotte will be the first to hear," said Richard, taking over from me whilst Roddie and I continued to hold our gaze. "I have asked Kirsty to marry me and she has not refused."

"Richard!" I said.

He looked at me. "You cannot deny it, can you?" he said.

I looked at him dumbly. Perhaps it was for the best. Then I turned to Roddie. I saw shock first, then disbelief and finally anger and I thought – I cannot bear it! Then Charlotte's voice broke in.

"Oh, how wonderful!" she said. "What a clever little thing you are, Kirsty! You'll be mistress of Blair Morach. Congratulations, Richard!"

I waited for Roddie's outburst but it did not come. He merely bowed from the waist and took my cold hand in his warm one and said, "I wish you all happiness, Kirsty, as I have always done."

A movement behind him caught my eye and for a moment Effie, in neat black with a white apron and cap, looked straight into my eyes. I felt a small shock-wave run through me at the venom in her eyes. I had forgotten that she was in love with Richard and I was filled with pity for her. I made to move towards her, but she turned away and I was helpless. I could not run after her. Then the first dance was announced.

It was, of course, The Falls of Morach, and as the pipers burst into full cry, Richard held his hand out to me and led me out to the middle of the hall, the other couples following behind.

"Do you know the reel?" I whispered.

Charlotte's voice came from behind me. "We learned it in the nursery," she said. "All the Munros did, though we might be a bit rusty."

I turned my head and caught a glimpse of her face sparkling up at Roddie, then the reel began. Scottish reels are not sedate affairs, not in the Highlands at any rate, and this was no exception. The kilts of the men swung as they whirled in and out of the sets, the gowns of the ladies swirling and billowing in time to the music. It was a reel that required the two top couples to dance together and, as we wove our way, the four of us, in and out of the complex of figures, I thought how the patterns of the reel mirrored our lives this last year.

Richard and Charlotte did indeed know the steps, but they did not dance the reel, not as Roddie and I did, with all our heritage behind us. And, as he moved towards me to claim me for our figures, I put my hands in his and we danced as one. His eyes, dark above the sparkling white of his cravat, never left my face and for that brief convergence I forgot everything but the music and the dance and Roddie. Then it was over, and Richard and I were weaving in and out of the dancers to the bottom of the set, leaving Roddie and Charlotte to partner another couple.

Roddie claimed me for only one dance, a strathspey, elegant and stately and measured in its pace. As he led me down the middle of the long line of dancers he said softly, "You're looking well, Kirsty."

I tried to smile my thanks, but something must have shown in my face for he breathed a muttered oath and his grip tightened to painfulness on my hand.

"No, dammit, you're not looking well," he said. "You look beautiful, untouchable, like a fey creature."

We moved to set to the top couple and it was a moment before we came together again, a moment to recollect myself.

"You're looking well yourself, Roddie," I said. "A stranger could be forgiven for thinking you were the young laird rather than Richard. You certainly look the part."

And he did, in his full Highland dress, the black jacket and the crisp white linen, and above, his eyes, never leaving mine.

A muscle tensed at the side of his mouth at my words.

"And would it make any difference if I were the young laird?" he said. "Is it the man you're marrying, Kirsty, or the laird?"

I almost said, "But I have not promised to marry him – I have only said 'perhaps' ". Then the dance took us apart again down the outside of the lines and I thought – let him think I have promised. Let him think I am marrying for position and money. Better that than the truth. I almost smiled. Mrs MacLelland would be proud of me. When we came together again he was calmer.

"What's wrong with Effie?" he said. "She looks different."

I was glad to change the subject.

"She's been strange these past weeks," I said. "I think she's mixing herself up in superstition and the like. Charlotte says she caught her making up potions and she hasn't looked at all well lately." I bit my lip. Should I mention my suspicion that Effie was pregnant, that this might explain why she had been brewing up potions?

His voice was harsh. "What superstitions?" he said.

I looked at him in surprise. "She had that book about the legends of Morach and the Druid Island," I replied. "It was full of nonsense about witchcraft and the like."

"I remember there was a copy in the library here," he said. "Where is it now?"

I was puzzled at his vehemence. "I don't know," I said. "I suppose Effie still has it. Why?"

"Because it's dangerous, that's why," he said.

"Dangerous?" I protested. "A whole lot of nonsense about the Druid Island? What's dangerous about the Druid Island?"

His eyes were as black as his grandmother's as he looked down at me and I felt the smile fade from my lips.

"Nothing," he said. "It's the things folk will believe that are dangerous."

I was reminded of Mrs MacLelland's words to me on the day of the blanket wash – it isn't the stories that make a place evil, she had said, but the foolishness of those that believe in them.

"I must talk to Effie," Roddie was saying. "Tonight."

There was an urgency in his voice that surprised me. Then the dance ended on a long skirling note and, with a swift bow, he was gone in the throng.

I would have gone after him but Richard was immediately at my side.

"Not very gentlemanly, leaving you here in the middle of the floor," he said.

I laughed. "Oh, Roddie never set himself up as a gentleman," I said.

"I can imagine," Richard said drily. "Where has he gone in such a hurry?"

"To find Effie," I said.

His eyes flickered towards me. "Effie? Whatever for?" he said.

I shrugged. "Oh, I don't know," I said. "She's upset. I suppose he's worried about her."

"Strange," he said.

"Not really," I replied. "After all, she's a Morach girl. We've known her all our lives."

He smiled at me. "You really do hang together here, don't you?" he said.

"We protect our own," I said, though why I chose those exact words, I could not say.

It was some time later that Charlotte grasped my arm from behind.

"Where's Roddie?" she said, her pretty mouth sulky.

"I don't know," I replied. "I haven't seen him for some time. Perhaps he's with Richard."

She tapped her foot impatiently. "I can't find Richard either," she said. "Where can they be?"

I shrugged. "Perhaps they've gone out for some fresh air," I said. "It's terribly hot in here now."

Fires had been lit in the enormous fireplaces at either end of the great hall and, with the energetic dancing, the air was almost stifling. A light leapt in Charlotte's eyes.

"He's gone to the ceilidh in the village," she said. "That's where I'll find him."

She turned swiftly away and it was my turn to grasp her arm.

"You can't do that, Charlotte," I said. "The village wouldn't like it. You're gentry. You'd only embarrass them if you intruded like that."

She faced me again. "The village!" she said scornfully. "Who cares about the village? If Roddie's there then I'm going."

I looked at her, determined, unable to think of anything but finding Roddie.

"But you'll be as good as running after him," I said. "The whole of Morach will know. Have you no pride, Charlotte?"

Her eyes were suddenly drowned in sadness. "No, Kirsty," she said. "Not where he's concerned."

I felt a wave of fondness for her. For all her faults, she loved Roddie.

"Then I'll come with you," I said. "You cannot go alone."

She nodded briefly and would have gone straight out into the frosty night, but I made her wait while I fetched our warm cloaks and together we slipped out of a side door and down to Morach.

The air was crisp, the full moon flooding the glen with light, but my feet in their inadequate dancing slippers were soon chilled and I was glad when we approached the lighted village hall. We could hear the sound of fiddles and laughter from some distance and the yellow radiance of the lamps was welcoming, promising warmth. I tried once more to dissuade Charlotte, nonetheless, but she would not listen though I saw her take a deep breath before she pushed open the door.

The chattering and music continued for a moment, the dancers whirled and passed, then, gradually, the noise died down, the music ceased and every face was turned towards us. She stood there, flushed but steady, not flinching before their eyes, then someone moved out of the crowd and Roddie was saying, "Miss Munro, it's honoured indeed we are by your presence and good of you to accompany Kirsty to the ceilidh."

I looked at him gratefully but his eyes were on Charlotte, compelling her to play her part, which she did with grace and dignity.

"I should not like to intrude," she said and that was all that was necessary.

At once there rose protestations on all sides and she was ushered into the room with many words of welcome. I was still standing in the open doorway and, as I turned to close the door against the frosty night, I let my glance range over the loch. The village hall stood on a slight rise and the moon shone clear on the waters of the loch. But it was not that which caught my attention. It was a light bobbing up and down on the Druid Island, like a lantern carried by someone walking over rough ground. I could not understand it. What would anyone be doing on Druid Island tonight of all nights when both village and castle were celebrating? Roddie was at my side, reaching across me to close the door.

"It's a terrible draught you're letting in, Kirsty," he said. "And you look frozen to the bone."

"There's a light on Druid Island," I said, not shifting my gaze and then, as if from nowhere, came the words, "Did you find Effie?"

There was a moment when neither of us moved, then he looked swiftly back into the room. Charlotte was the centre of attention, but I saw her eyes flick momentarily towards us. The rest paid no heed.

"Quickly," said Roddie, giving me a push. "I may need your help."

We were out of the door and running down towards the lych-gate, though neither of us, I'm sure, could have put a name to the fear that possessed us.

He had untied the boat and handed me in when there was a quick step behind us and

Charlotte said, "Where are you going? What's happening?"

Roddie cursed softly. "Did anyone see you leave?" he asked.

Charlotte looked doubtful. "I don't think so," she said. "The dancing is quite wild in there. I slipped out after you."

"Then get in the boat," he said. "Rather that than have you alarm the whole village."

She did as she was told at once and without fuss but, as we approached the island by the long sweep round the undertow, she said again, "What on earth is going on?"

"Hush!" whispered Roddie fiercely. "Sound carries over water."

The air was so still that the sound of the oars plashing in the water was overloud in my ears, though I knew Roddie was making as little noise as possible and, when the bottom scraped on the shore of the island, I heard him curse softly to himself. We carried the boat up on to dry sand rather than drag it and, as silently as we could, made our way up to the ring of oaks that surrounded the green centre and the Druid Stone.

Chapter 15

The moon was full and bright over the circle of stones, casting its merciless light on the scene below. I felt the breath dry in my throat and heard Charlotte whimper beside me. The sound was more like a wounded animal than a human being. Then all was silence again except for the soft sound of waves washing on the shore behind. We stared, all three of us rigid with horror, at the Druid Stone.

Effie was there. She lay unconscious across the Druid Stone. She was stripped to her shift and it was pitifully obvious what had caused her distress in recent weeks. I looked at the small mound the thin shift could not disguise. My suspicions had been correct. She was indeed pregnant. But that seemed irrelevant as we stood there on the Druid Island.

Irrelevant, because over her stood Richard, his arm raised. In his hand the blade of a knife glittered wickedly in the frosty light. The small green-covered book lay open in front of him on the stone and he was muttering words from it. Then his fingers seemed to tighten on the knife handle and he made a slow, sweeping gesture as he plunged the knife towards that small white body.

"STOP!"

The word rang out, clear in the still air, as Roddie leapt forward on to the ridge. Richard's eyes came up to meet his. I covered my face for a moment, unable to believe what I saw, for they were mad eyes, Richard's and yet not Richard's. When I took my hands away I felt a sob torn from me as I realized that Roddie's command had stopped him in the act. I felt Charlotte's hand grope for mine. I held it tightly, unable to take my eyes from the scene before me. Richard was looking at Roddie in a puzzled fashion.

"I have said the incantation," he said and his voice was horribly reasonable. "I cannot stop now."

"You must," said Roddie steadily, calmly. But he did not move again. The knife was too near to Effie's breast. He could not afford to antagonize Richard.

"You don't understand," said Richard. "She must die. She will tell Kirsty that the child is mine and then Kirsty will not marry me after all. And Kirsty *must* marry me." He spread his hands wide and I stifled a sigh of relief as I watched the knife move away from Effie. "You see what I am without Kirsty," he said. "You must see that Effie has to die."

Roddie took a step forward and at once the blade flashed and the knife was poised once again over its victim.

"Don't come any closer," Richard said, "or I will kill her at once. As it is, I do not mind discussing the subject with you. You see, it does not matter if I tell you, for now you must also die. I should have killed you that time on the moor. My aim is not usually so bad. I cannot understand why I did not."

"I moved too quickly," said Roddie, and there was a grim humour in his tone.

Richard looked interested. "Then you knew it was intentional," he said. "I wondered at the time."

"I was not certain," said Roddie. "I only suspected."

Richard nodded sympathetically. "Awkward for you," he said. "I knew, of course, that you were trying to keep the 'understanding' you had with Kirsty secret, trying to throw me off the scent by flirting with Charlotte."

"I was reluctant to push you too far," Roddie said amiably. "I did not want to risk your jealousy."

Richard laughed. "Oh, I was jealous all right," he said. "I only had to see Kirsty's eyes when she looked at you to know that she loved you. I knew it even before she knew it herself." He put his head on one side. "I wish I'd had the nerve to try again after I botched it on the moor."

I felt I must be going mad myself to be listening to such a conversation in such circumstances.

"However, I shall not miss this time," Richard went on. "I brought this along in case of any interference. It does not do to be too confident." And from his pocket he drew a pistol and laid it gently on the stone beside Effie.

She moaned softly as the butt of the pistol touched her and I had not realized until then how afraid I had been that she was already dead.

"It's a pity," said Richard, smoothing her hair gently, for all the world as if he were soothing a child back to sleep. "I had it all worked out. Effie needn't have died if she hadn't been so stupid as to threaten me, and she has been so useful with her gossip and half-remembered stories. Poor girl, she had it all wrong but she has been useful. I shall be sorry in a way to kill her." He looked up and smiled pleasantly at Roddie. "It was so simple," he said. "You see, I made Charlotte tell Kirsty that Jamie Strachan was your father and, of course, being Kirsty, she was unlikely ever to repeat that to you. But it did mean that she could not marry you. I knew she would turn to me. I have always been different with Kirsty. Different. . .” he repeated almost to himself. “You must see why I need her.”

“Charlotte?” Roddie said and I felt her hand move convulsively in mine. But I was curiously unsurprised by Richard’s next words.

“Charlotte has always been afraid of me,” he said. “We were in the nursery together, you see. I think perhaps she thought that what she suffered were simply boyish pranks, that I would grow out of them, but when she was forced by circumstances to come and live with us she learned differently. I had not changed, only grown more subtle.” He smiled with pride. “It’s important to learn your victim’s weaknesses,” he continued. “You were Charlotte’s weakness, Roddie. She was always afraid that I would repeat that incident on the moor. Silly girl! I would not have been so stupid. But I would have found another way if she had not agreed to help me. And she knew it.” He smoothed Effie’s hair again, almost protectively. “Now Effie’s weakness was superstition,” he said. “It was not difficult to persuade her to come here tonight. It is Hallowmas, after all, and she was desperate to see me alone to persuade me to marry her. The mistake she made was in trying to threaten me. That I will not tolerate.”

His voice had risen dangerously, but one thing rang in my mind so that I barely heard Roddie's voice as it whipped the still air. It was a lie! Roddie was not my father's son. But if he was not, then whose son was he?

"You know who I am then?" Roddie said as if in answer to my thoughts.

Richard smiled up at him, his voice dropping again. "I have had my suspicions. No more," he said. Then he laughed. "May I call you brother?"

I saw Roddie flinch and Richard laughed again with what appeared to be real amusement.

"It's a pity I have to kill you," he said, fingering his gun as it lay glinting in the moonlight, "especially when you are my only brother and so recently found. But then there is a precedent for it, is there not? Cain killed Abel just as I shall kill you," and he lifted the gun and pointed it straight at Roddie.

As the shot rang out, I moved instinctively, without thought, wrenching my hand from Charlotte's. As I sprang on to the ridge, a branch caught on my cloak and tore it from my shoulders and I found myself walking calmly down towards Richard. Roddie had flung himself sideways and I was past him before he could get to his feet. Richard and I stood looking at each other, the gun now turned towards me. I saw surprise and wonder in his eyes, and then panic as his glance flickered towards the book that lay before him.

"It cannot be," he said. "It is only a legend."

Understanding came slowly as I realized the picture I made, standing there in the ancient place, my hair rippling about my shoulders and the thin sea-green chiffon of the gown floating about me. A selkie, a sea creature. No doubt there were stories of such creatures in the book.

"For a moment I thought you were Kirsty," Richard said. "But, of course, you can take any shape you wish. Don't harm me!" he said. "I need to do this. Don't harm me!"

He had slipped finally over the edge of sanity, his eyes fixed on mine, pleading, believing me to be some kind of spirit. I stretched out my hands, palms upwards, and slowly he moved forward and into them put first the gun and then the knife.

They lay heavy in my hands and, as I looked at him, I felt the tears stand in my eyes. Richard! So amusing. So gentle always to me. And so flawed. I realized now why I had always felt wary of him. This was the Richard that lay behind the mask, the Richard I had half glimpsed from time to time but never fully understood. But at that moment I felt only pity for him.

"Richard!" I said and it was as if I had struck him.

"Kirsty?" he said wonderingly. "It *is* you." Then his face changed and he began to back away from me. "No!" he screamed. "No, you cannot know this! For you I have always been different."

Roddie was by my side, taking the gun and the knife from my hands, and Richard looked at him. All at once he seemed quite sane, the old Richard.

"So, you have won after all, brother," he said. "But I shall go to hell my own road!" And he turned and plunged up the farther ridge. I made to follow but found Roddie's arms around me, holding me back. At the top of the rise, Richard stopped and turned to me.

"Goodbye, Kirsty," he said. "With you I could have been good."

I felt the tears coursing down my cheeks as I looked at him standing there like an engaging small boy. Then he was gone and Roddie was saying, "It is better this way, believe me, Kirsty."

I shivered in his arms and Charlotte came and put my cloak around me. None of us said a word when we heard the splash as Richard entered the water.

Chapter 16

Effie was still unconscious. Roddie picked her up and we bundled her in her cloak. We found the boat Richard had used and Charlotte sat in that with Effie's head cradled in her lap, whilst we towed them towards the shore. Roddie spoke only once. As I looked across the calm water, so deceptive, between the island and the shore, he said, "He knew about the undertow. It was his choice."

I nodded, but I would never erase from my mind that last picture of him, so engaging, so pleasant. That other Richard was a stranger to me.

We set Richard's boat adrift when we reached the shore and I watched it move over the quiet water until it wheeled suddenly in the current. Then I turned away and followed Roddie up to the village. Old Mrs MacLelland made no comment and asked no questions when we arrived on her doorstep with Effie sleeping still.

"She's been given a strong dose of laudanum," she said. "I doubt whatever's happened to her has done the baby any good, but leave her with me. Tell her mother she fainted at the ceilidh and I've taken her in. She wouldn't be the first."

That was all. No doubt Roddie would tell her the whole story. I wouldn't have been surprised to learn she knew it already but then she was no ordinary woman.

Roddie walked Charlotte and me up to the castle, a more subdued Charlotte than I had ever seen. As he left us he took her hand.

"I blame you for nothing," he said. "Don't blame yourself." But she would not meet his eyes. And to me, "Well, Kirsty, I'll ask you again. Is it the laird or the man?"

I did meet his eyes. "They're the same thing, are they not?" I said. "But it's always been the man."

He left us then to go to the Laird and we went silently to bed. There was nothing to be said.

Richard's body was washed up on the other side of the loch the next day, and the village said it was a terrible tragedy and he must have been full of whisky to be out in a boat at that time of night. Effie remembered nothing after she and Richard arrived on the island where he had promised to "walk round the Druid Stone" with her, and she had enough sense to keep her doings to herself, enough sense or a good dose of

Mrs MacLelland. She lost the child, which wasn't surprising, considering. But it was the Laird that my heart went out to. Roddie told him everything, and when next I saw him he looked older and greyer than I had ever seen him.

"You know it all, Kirsty?" he said when he called me to the library.

I nodded. "There's no need to go over it," I said. "It'll only distress you."

He shook his head. "There are some things I must say to you, explain to you," he said. "Hear me out, Kirsty, or I'll not rest easy."

I sat down and he began.

"Your father and I went back a long way," he said. "Right back as far as I remember. We were the best of friends, the best, but we both wanted Catriona MacLelland and it made a rift between us. Oh, she was a bonny lass and I was smitten, but it was your father she really loved, only she was dazzled by being sought after by the young laird as I was then, and I was set on marrying her. She would have gone back to your father if I had given her time to think, but I didn't. I took her to the Druid Island, and I walked round the Druid Stone with her and we lay a night on the island together. It wasn't as uncommon then as it is now and I considered myself married to her. But then your father went away to Glasgow and she began to see that maybe she'd made the wrong choice.

"Then my own father had me up in front of him one day and told me the estate was in a sore way, and I'd have to marry and bring some money into it. I couldn't tell him about Catriona. Besides, she was regretting it herself and we'd only lain together the once. So I said I would. I didn't care. Catriona was the only girl I wanted and she didn't want me and no matter how you looked at it, neither the law nor the church would consider us married."

Here he paused and his gaze shifted to the fire. "The woman I did marry was pretty enough," he said, and now there was a harshness in his tone, "but I soon learned what the bargain was. There was insanity in her family. Not that it showed in her, but she knew of it and didn't tell me. I found out after Richard was born. At first I thought it was just temper – his rages, his cruelties – for he could be the pleasantest, most amusing boy at other times. But then we'd be asked to take him away from yet another school until finally we got a tutor at home for him.

"Poor Charlotte suffered badly for it when she came to visit, but even I didn't realize how badly. She's been talking to me about it for the first time."

His head drooped in his hands. "Then Richard was sent down from Oxford – there was a shooting accident, only there was more than a suspicion it wasn't an accident. And there was some secret society he started. It stopped short of scandal but only just. I don't know the whole story myself, but there was talk of black magic and such nonsense. I thought that he would be safe here but I was wrong, Kirsty."

He was silent for so long that I was forced to speak.

"You did what you could," I said. "After all, he's your son."

"And what of my other son?" he said. "The one I didn't know I had. Catriona never wrote to me, no more did her mother. I didn't know there was a child. Even when I came back this time it never entered my head that Roddie was mine. I knew I had been the first with Catriona, but thought – God help me! that maybe your father had come back..."

"My mother thought the same," I said. "At least she was never sure Roddie was not my father's child. And yet Mrs MacLelland has told me now that she assured her again and again that it wasn't true."

"She didn't tell her who it really was though," he said.

I shook my head. "No," I said. "That was the trouble. Because she refused to tell her that, Mother could never be certain."

He shook his head. "It's been a sorry business," he said. "And my fault, all of it. But I'm trying to make amends. I had a talk with Mrs MacLelland a while back and she told me then, for I asked her outright about Catriona, but I couldn't recognize Roddie for fear of what it would do to Richard. I tried to help him in other ways. But he's proud as the devil, Kirsty, and he's not taken kindly to what I said to him today, though he holds no grievance towards me."

"He wouldn't," I said.

The Laird leaned forward, his eyes fixed on me.

"I want to adopt him legally", he said, "as my son. He's a son any man would be proud of and it's his due and his mother's. I want him to have Morach, to be the laird after me, and I want you to persuade him. You're the only one who can."

I looked at him, an old man suddenly, and I remembered that he had been my father's friend and his life had not been easy.

"I'll try," I said.

"That's all I ask," he replied.

I left him still staring into the fire and, as I went out of the room, Charlotte passed me, coming in.

"I've made my peace with Roddie, Kirsty," she said. "He's waiting for you. He says you'll know where to find him. Now I have to make my peace with you."

I put my hands on her shoulders and kissed her cheek. "There's no need for that," I said. "I understand. Your uncle has explained everything."

She flushed. "I'll be leaving soon," she said, "and I won't be coming back to Morach. I'm sorry, Kirsty, and I wish you happiness."

I let her go. Only time could heal the hurt she was feeling.

I found Roddie down by the shore, looking out towards the Druid Island.

"I know now why you were so angry when I joked about walking round the Druid Stone," I said. "I suppose you have always known who your father was."

"Ever since I can remember," he said, rising to meet me. "And I've always known I could not say."

"Your grandmother has an unusual regard for the truth," I said.

He smiled at that. "It's taken a lifetime learning she's right," he said. "At first I just accepted I must tell no one. Then, as I grew older, I was determined to prove I was legitimate. I thought the law that said they were not married when they had pledged themselves to each other was wrong."

"And that was what made you determined to take up the law?" I said.

He nodded, then grinned. "The trouble is, I started to get interested in it for its own sake and somehow it didn't seem to matter any more that I should rightly be heir to Blair Morach."

"You can be now," I said.

He shook his head. "I don't need it now," he said. "I have you. Or is it the Laird of Morach that you want after all, Kirsty?"

I laughed. "Come and I'll show you," I said and his arms were around me, and all the hurt and pain of the last weeks were washed away by his kiss.

He lifted his head at last. "It's the man after all, Kirsty Strachan," he said, "and that's all I need and all I ever will need."

"The Laird has needs," I said. "You may not need Blair Morach, but he has no other heir and he has a wrong he wants to set right. He's an old man, Roddie, and he's your father."

He looked at me a long moment, then he said, "Those could be my grandmother's words."

I laughed. "In that case," I said, "there's nothing to discuss."

And together we turned our backs on the Druid Island and I walked up to Morach and around me were the arms of the young laird.

Historical Note

The word "Druid" means "knowledge of the oak tree". The Druids themselves were Celtic priests and were members of the learned class among the ancient Celts. They also acted as teachers and judges. They studied ancient verse, natural philosophy, astronomy and the lore of the gods. Their principal belief was that the soul was immortal and passed at death from one person into another. They offered human sacrifice for those who were gravely ill or in danger of death in battle. In the early period their main rituals and ceremonies were held in clearings in the forest and they considered the oak and mistletoe to be sacred. The earliest records of the Druids date from the third century BC. With the coming of Christianity, the Druidic religion disappeared, but for centuries afterwards their influence on folk culture could still be felt.

Down to recent times, even earlier prehistoric remains such as standing stones and grave slabs have attracted superstitious belief in the Highlands of Scotland. Bargains were often concluded by the parties clasping hands through "holed stones". Many stones, like the holed stones in Kintyre, were associated with marriage customs. Healing stones and healing pools can be found all over Scotland. These were still regarded as magical centuries after the Druids had gone. In a society which relied on natural remedies, those who were skilled in herbal medicine (usually women) were sometimes regarded as witches or "wise women". In the remoter parts of the Scottish Highlands in the last century natural medicine and folklore customs often went hand in hand.

In the middle of the nineteenth century the Highlands were changing. Queen Victoria's love of Balmoral, the coming of the railways, better roads and a general interest in folklore brought many a land-owner back from the South. A Highland estate became a fashionable asset. But, for the communities themselves, change was slow. The old religions of pre-Christian times survived in some ways still, handed down as custom and superstition. And so, in the more isolated parts of the Highlands, it was perfectly possible to find Christianity and superstition existing side by side – and often superstition was the more powerful of the two.

.